Penguin Books
Zee & Co.

Edna O'Brien was born in the West
of Ireland and now lives in London
with her two sons. She has written
*The Country Girls, Girl with Green Eyes,
Girls in their Married Bliss, August is a
Wicked Month, Casualties of Peace, A
Pagan Place, Zee & Co* (all in Penguins),
and *The Love Object* – short stories.

Edna O'Brien

Zee & Co.

Penguin Books

Penguin Books Ltd, Harmondsworth,
Middlesex, England
Penguin Books Inc., 7110 Ambassador Road,
Baltimore, Maryland 21207, U.S.A.
Penguin Books Australia Ltd, Ringwood,
Victoria, Australia

First published by Weidenfeld & Nicolson 1971
Published in Penguin Books 1971
Copyright © Edna O'Brien, 1971

Made and printed in Great Britain by
Cox & Wyman Ltd,
London, Reading and Fakenham
Set in Monotype Baskerville

For Thea Porter

Author's Note

Zee & Co. was written as an original screenplay. I have edited it slightly to take out the film technicalities and make it more readable as a book. Of course, by the time the film appears, it may differ from changes made in the course of shooting, but the book as it appears here represents my intention.

Edna O'Brien
September 1970

Chapter One

She sang while she played, Zee did. Always – 'My love is a red red prick.' Robert and Zee are playing the final point in a game of table tennis. Robert misses. Zee lets out a shriek of joy. They have been having a tournament, this last game is the decisive one. She goes to the board and chalks up the result, then throws the chalk down, wipes her hand to free it of dust and heads for the door.

ZEE. What do I get? The boot?

Robert picks up the various balls and puts them in the nets. Zee can be heard humming as she goes tearing up the stairs. Robert, about to leave the room, returns and with the end of his shirt, wipes the chalked record off the board. He is quiet, sad almost.

Zee, in a brassière and pants, is looking into her vast wardrobe of clothes. She takes out a dress of ostrich feathers and holds it up to herself, viewing herself in the mirror. She takes out a shortie nightdress and puts it on. In the nightdress she runs out of her room and into Robert's bedroom. He has begun to change. She picks up a heater and leaves with it.

ZEE. It's Arctic.

ROBERT. If you insist on going around naked . . .

ZEE. What are you wearing, a cloak and dagger?

ROBERT. What do you suggest?

ZEE. Something that will see you through till four in the morning.

ROBERT. I'm not staying out till four in the morning, I have to work tomorrow.

ZEE. Then wear something orthodox – a suit.

Zee runs from the room.

ROBERT. What?

Zee bangs the door.

ROBERT. Thanks a lot, Baby.

Zee enters her own room, plugs in the heater and then gets a quilt which she puts round herself, slowly and carefully. She then sits at her dressing-table, plugs in various lights and commences to do her face. Robert enters.

ROBERT. Is it black tie or isn't it?

ZEE. How would I know? Ring and find out. And she'll say some are wearing black tie and some are not. All very democratic.

Robert stands for a minute and it looks as if he might hit her but then he doesn't. As he goes away she concentrates with great self-love on the painting of her eyebrows.

Robert is standing against the wall with a certain forbearance, whistling. Zee emerges from her bedroom dressed very extravagantly.

ZEE [*pouting*] Oh not that shirt. I want you to wear the one I gave you.

ROBERT. It doesn't fit. You had a midget in mind.

ZEE. I love you in bright colours. Peacock. I love you anyhow.

She links him as they go down the stairs.

ZEE. Let's go somewhere on our own.

ROBERT. We can't do that at the last minute. Gladys would have forty fits.

ZEE. She relies on you, they all rely on you, the female sex.

Chapter Two

Zee and Robert enter Gladys's hallway. Zee ignores the servant who offers to take her wrap. She swathes it around herself more dramatically. They walk through the hall to the sitting-room where there are about twenty people. The room is beautifully and sumptuously appointed, the people also. They seem to complement the various drawings, paintings and tapestries that deck the walls. In the centre of the room is a three-way 'love' seat, noticeably empty. Gladys, the hostess, comes forward to greet them. She kisses Robert on either cheek.

GLADYS. My angel.

ROBERT [*biffing her*] You've got your fake jewellery on again.

GLADYS [*to Zee*] Horrid man ... how do you control him?

Zee does a punching movement with closed fist.

GLADYS [*offhand to Zee*] Pretty, you look.

Zee walks away. She approaches a young man, Brig.

ZEE. Well, here we are again ... [*She touches his dress shirt*] Back from the cleaners.

Zee, having got his attention, then passes him by

to engage another man, Troy, who is bearded.

ZEE. I bet you don't know what a byssus is . . .

TROY. I don't actually.

ZEE [*grasping his beard*] Beard. Having large silky byssus or beard . . .

Zee sees the long buffet table in the rear.

ZEE. At least we don't have to sit down, we can circulate . . . last week I sat next to some creep, asked me where I lived, asked if we'd got a beautiful staircase, yeh, I said, great for hangings.

She laughs to herself.

TROY. What do you come to parties for?

ZEE. The booze . . . the intrigues.

TROY. And your husband?

ZEE. Oh, he chats the birds . . .

TROY. It doesn't worry you?

Zee shakes her head, she looks at her legs, her ankles, her attire, her jewellery, assured of them and that they are hers. Gladys is also looking at herself in one of her own mirrored rings and at the same time talking to Robert, in a breathless whisper.

GLADYS. I want advice, there're some African pieces coming up at Sotheby's . . . well, Nigerian to be exact . . . they're for the rose garden, the place is grotty once the roses go.

Stella enters from the hallway. She is singularly well dressed. She stands on the threshold. Robert observes her. From a few feet behind, Zee observes her and does something to adjust her wrap, to make herself a little more bizarre.

ROBERT [*to Gladys*] You shall have it . . . then we'll

have a very smart lunch. Who's the . . . guest?

Gladys becomes aware of Stella, and frowns just before smiling.

GLADYS. That's darling Stella.

Robert touches Gladys's elbow to urge her in Stella's direction.

ROBERT. Come on, effect an introduction.

GLADYS [*not budging*] Who told me he had settled down and was getting eight hours sleep a night?

ROBERT. That was during one of my depressions.

GLADYS. Aren't they agony . . .

ROBERT. What is she . . . a lady of leisure?

GLADYS. My dear, she dresses everybody. [*In an autocratic voice and curling her finger*] Stella dear, somebody who doesn't know you.

Gladys and Robert cross to join Stella. Zee breaks away from Troy and takes a few steps in their direction, watches, alone.

STELLA. I thought it was going to be a small gathering.

GLADYS. But they're all darling people. This is Robert.

ROBERT [*to Stella*] Do you need a bodyguard?

STELLA. Yes, I mean no.

ROBERT. Well now, you've broken the ice.

Robert gestures to a pendant she is wearing and almost touches her throat. The action is reflex and done before he realizes its import. Zee sees it. Robert then makes a point of touching the pendant itself, simulating great interest in it.

14

ROBERT. What is that?

STELLA. It's a Koran case.

ROBERT. It's dented.

STELLA. I believe I bit it.

Zee stands at Stella's back.

ZEE. You'd like my family, they're all doctors.

STELLA. What makes you think I like doctors?

ZEE. It's written all over you . . . your injuries.

Gladys shudders and walks away. Robert looks at Stella. Zee exhales steadily.

ROBERT. Can't see it myself.

The look is a fraction longer than is wise.

ZEE. He wouldn't know, he's an architect.

Stella turns from Robert to Zee.

STELLA. I know he's an architect. I've heard of him and his domes.

ZEE. It's not easy being married to a giant.

ROBERT [*nudging Stella*] Or a midget.

STELLA. It's not easy, anyhow.

ZEE. Huh-huh, elegy time.

ROBERT [*to Stella*] What do you do?

ZEE. She's a dress designer, very smart.

ROBERT [*to Stella*] Do I strike you as a well-dressed man?

Stella looks him over, shakes her head, wanly.

STELLA. No.

Zee goes off. She has had enough it would seem. Robert moves a fraction nearer to Stella and lowers his voice.

ROBERT. You will have to take me in hand.

STELLA. Clothes are such a personal thing.

ROBERT. That's what I mean – Who designed your place?

STELLA. I designed it.

ROBERT. I would have given you a cut.

STELLA. Too late.

Zee grabs two plates of food from a waiter and returns to where Robert and Stella are. Robert makes a face of disdain at the food. Zee hands a plate to Stella. Stella has to put her bag on her arm to accept the plate. She is a bit flustered.

ZEE. There was hot and cold. I took the liberty of getting you the hot, because you can always have the cold for a second helping.

Zee has the knife and fork ready but Stella has no more free hands. Zee indicates the love seat which is in the centre of the floor and she waits for Stella to go first. Robert gives Zee a darting look. As they cross the floor Gladys calls out to Stella.

GLADYS. I'm getting you lots of lovely customers.

Robert hurries down the room to the conservatory and taps a friend to ask for a game of snooker.

Stella and Zee appoint themselves on the love seat. Stella drapes her dress around her legs. Robert is chalking his cue and looking in Stella's direction.

ZEE. I hope he doesn't lose, he's a bad loser.

STELLA. Quite a gathering.

ZEE. Ever notice she has one of everything, one actor, one painter, one faith healer, the bankers and their spouses of course.

STELLA. She's alright, we all guzzle her wine.

ZEE. I haven't heard that word for years. That dates us. She guzzles out of a silver mug. Crafty. You can't get through to her after eleven in the morning. The words are beginning to go, shlur ... [*She mimes a drunken woman*] She tells Robert everything, even about having her face lifted, asked his advice.

STELLA [*touching her cheekbones*] It'll be my turn soon for that.

ZEE. Now you know who to ask. – Me.

A Siamese cat sidles towards them and as Zee bends down to pick it up she becomes aware of Stella's tremor. Stella shivers and turns away.

ZEE. Are you allergic?

STELLA. No, just terrified.

ZEE. You don't know what you're missing.

Zee gets up and opens the door of a cupboard in which there are ornaments and slings the cat in there. The cat miaows.

STELLA. We should have brought our embroidery.

ZEE. Yes. He's a bad loser. Also a miser. Men from poor backgrounds never get over it, do they? He keeps turning down the thermostat, our house is plebeian. Why am I telling you this, it must be because I like you, because you're so sympathetic. He didn't buy me a wedding ring, borrowed his sister's. We got the weirdest wedding presents. You know one thing we got. A collapsible waste-paper basket in leather, green leather. Did you get nice wedding presents?

STELLA. I eloped.

ZEE. Good for you. Where is he?

STELLA. He's in the country.

Stella suddenly rises and goes out of the room and hurries up the stairs.

ZEE [*to Gladys*] Oh, that's quick.

GLADYS. What on earth did you say?

ZEE. Just telling her about myself, fragments.

GLADYS. Did you know she told me once that she's prone to weeping when something nice happens.

ZEE [*making a vomit sound*] Eugh . . . eugh.

Stella closes the door of Gladys's bedroom and puts her back to it. She is in a panic and close to tears.

Robert taps on the door. He coughs. He calls in a whisper.

ROBERT. Stella . . .

Stella just stands there crying and does not answer.

ROBERT. Are you there?

Stella shakes her head back and forth, crying to herself.

Zee follows Robert half way up the stairs and calls to him.

ZEE. Robert . . . We're all going to go dancing, that's the latest.

ROBERT. I'm not going dancing, I'm going home.

ZEE. Me want Bobby . . . in me arms . . . gliding.

ROBERT [*in an audible and fairly disappointed whisper to Stella*] I only wanted to have another look at you, that was all.

Chapter Three

Robert and Stella are sitting in a booth at Hennekey's Bar. There is champagne in a tub. As they drink Robert is showing a rather large watch to Stella.

ROBERT. First day in years I wore a watch, that's what you've done to me, made me think of the blasted time.

STELLA. I feel I must tell you. – It's expensive. I only eat the choicest things apart from cabbage.

ROBERT. Zee likes cold cabbage too. Late at night.

STELLA. I knew we had something in common.

Robert leans over and touches her wrist as if feeling her pulse.

ROBERT. Everyone has two types and one is true and one is false.

STELLA. How can one tell?

ROBERT. One can tell by the skin, by the touch . . .

STELLA [*humorously*] And by the eyes, the windows of the soul.

Robert laughs, then kisses her and they rise, and leave, most of the champagne undrunk. Robert signals to the barman to charge it to his account.

Outside, as they walk along they are approached

by a young girl who is remarkably like Zee. The young girl propositions Robert by walking directly in his line and then shrugs as she passes him by.

ROBERT. Lovely girl.

STELLA. Think so?

ROBERT. A humming bird.

STELLA. Thick ankles.

ROBERT. Don't tell me you're jealous.

STELLA. I don't like people encroaching on my man.

ROBERT. Congratulations.

He starts to kiss her.

ROBERT. You like to be kissed there?

STELLA. No.

ROBERT. There?

STELLA. No.

ROBERT. There?

STELLA. No.

ROBERT. Liar.

STELLA. I lied to your wife. I told her my husband was in the country. – Whereas in fact he's dead . . .

ROBERT [*with a smile*] That makes you a widow.

STELLA. And a liar.

They walk again. There is a wind and Robert walks in front of her with his jacket open to protect her from it.

STELLA. Where are we going?

ROBERT. Do you want me to take you to dinner? Or do you want to cook me an egg?

STELLA. I don't know.

ROBERT. Why don't you cook me an egg?

Stella is doubtful.

ROBERT. Because you can't cook.

STELLA. No. I'd drop things.

He kisses her again.

STELLA. You know how it is. You get over being silly and then you're silly again.

ROBERT I watched you come in the hall. You looked for, destiny.

STELLA. Break the ice, you said.

ROBERT. I touched you then.

In the taxi they maintain a perpetual embrace. The driver who is watching them in his mirror is frowning at his own deprivation and saying 'Cor' from time to time. They emerge from the taxi and enter a hotel. Robert turns round and smiles at her through the glass of the revolving doors, gropes with his hands and his mouth on the glass as if he were a mute. She smiles at him but cannot join in the impersonation that he is doing.

Stella and Robert are seated in the middle of the hotel's vast dining-room at a small table. Robert is feeding her grissticks on which he has put lashings of butter.

STELLA. Do you have a brother?

ROBERT. Yes.

STELLA. Would you introduce us?

ROBERT. I've got three. Brothers.

STELLA. What do they do?

ROBERT. One's an ex-builder like me, one's a business-man and one breaks in horses in California.

STELLA. I'll have him.

ROBERT. Do you ride?

STELLA. Only when I go away on grand weekends. Do you?

ROBERT. No, my wife does.

STELLA. That needn't stop you riding.

ROBERT. I can't let you meet my brother. [*He spits on her hand*] You're bespoke.

Stella chews whatever she is eating and shakes her head very resolutely.

STELLA. I'm not. I'm not falling in love with a married man, not again.

ROBERT. Have you been?

STELLA. Everyone has been in love with a married man, and it's hell.

ROBERT. It depends on how married he is. I married my wife because she had no parents, nothing to fall back on. I thought it would give her a basis.

STELLA. And did it?

Robert puts both hands round his own neck in a choking gesture.

ROBERT. We battled throughout the entire honeymoon. I cracked my skull diving, so I was indisposed. We fought so much that the people above us and below us and on either side asked if we could be made to leave.

STELLA. Maybe you like a fight.

Robert drops his knife and fork and grabs hold of her very sharply.

ROBERT. So that's what you're after.

STELLA. I'm talking about you.

ROBERT. But the colour has come to your cheeks.

STELLA. Because you're digging into me, with your architect nails.

ROBERT. That's what I like, less of the old adoration and a bit of gumption.

STELLA. You thought I was very ladylike, didn't you?

ROBERT. I thought no such thing. You didn't fool me.

STELLA. I've singed a few people in my time.

ROBERT [comically] Feathers?

STELLA. No, wings.

Robert lets go of her hands and resumes his dinner, a little more delighted, conditioned as he is to constant battling.

ROBERT. It was in Corfu. Room 184, Hotel Palace. I'll take you there if you like.

STELLA. I'd like.

ROBERT. I'll take you there.

They eat, chewing very consciously, silent for a bit.

Chapter Four

It is a little like a temple, oriental clothes, long robes, embroidered cushions with small mirrors between the embroideries, shells that chime, mobiles, bales of exotic cloth, a long sofa to stretch out on, shawls over each chair, and on the walls, beads, masks, curiosities.

Zee enters in very contrasting gear – boots and a leopardskin cat suit. She enters very quietly and when she sees the sort of place she's in, joins her hands to indicate a gesture of prayer, and closes her eyes to induce meditation. She sniffs the air. She touches a few robes approvingly and walks to the back of the shop to another room which is much smaller and which is full of half-completed clothes, dresses on dummies, chaos. Stella is sitting on a stool eating a sandwich from a paper. Zee enters on tiptoe. Stella has her back to her. Zee takes stock of the situation, nods her head in total approval, puts her fingers in her mouth to execute a shrill umpire's whistle. Stella turns round, sees Zee and gets up, flurried.

ZEE. I told you I'd see you again. I knew I would. Except that you didn't believe me did you?

Stella proffers the paper bag in which there is a sandwich.

STELLA. Have some lunch.

ZEE. Lovely. I forget to eat most days. [*Sees a box of buns*] I see you have a sweet tooth.

Zee starts to eat very heartily and Stella applies herself to tidying. While eating, Zee is turning the handle of a sewing machine and enjoying the sound that it makes.

ZEE. I saw a funny thing just now – a man at a long table and opposite were six or seven ladies, all Indian. What do you think they were?

STELLA. Indians.

ZEE. But the relationship?

STELLA. Sisters maybe.

ZEE. Do you have a sister?

STELLA. No.

ZEE. Nor me. I wish I had. I'd like to have a sister, to confide in. – Very nice your place, very tasteful. Guess why I'm here.

Stella looks at her quite assuredly and shakes her head. It is here for the first time that we are conscious of Stella's gift for being abstracted. She shakes her head and turns to do something to a garment on a stand.

STELLA. I'm not clairvoyant this morning. I never am on Mondays.

ZEE [*touching Stella on the shoulders*] I want you to dress me from head to toe. I want to be a product of your imagination. I want when people see me that they say Snap and think it's you.

Stella walks to the shop, followed by Zee. From the downstairs Gavin, a boy of about twenty, who is

Stella's assistant, comes up, carrying some georgette dresses.

ZEE. Lovely. Boys as well.

Zee grabs one of the dresses from him and holds it to herself.

GAVIN. That one's sold.

ZEE. That never deterred me.

Stella takes it from Zee, handing her another.

STELLA. Green ought to be a good colour for you. What are you, an eight?

ZEE. I'm fatter than you think. I'm a ten.

Zee starts to undress there and then in the middle of the shop. Gavin goes into the other room. Zee is in her pants and brassière and obligingly Stella moves one of the screens in front of her, to shield her from the world.

STELLA [*smiling*] Now, we don't want everybody knowing you're a ten do we?

Zee gets into the dress and looks at herself in the mirror which is hanging on the back of the screen. She is tugging at the zip when Stella comes to her rescue.

ZEE. Crikey. Who's going to do this for me?

STELLA. Your husband.

ZEE. But when I'm not there. Or he's not there. It sometimes happens. – We're fine, we're better than anyone else we know, we go coasting along and in the middle of the night, if my teeth chatter he holds on to me and vice versa. [*Touching the dress*] I'll have this. [*And selecting another off a hanger*] And I quite like that.

Zee gets out of one dress and into another. Stella

closes her eyes and Zee closes hers too. Zee laughs at this. The dress is much too big for her. Stella shakes her head.

ZEE. But I want it, it's the right material, voile or something.

STELLA. It would be a pity to hack it.

ZEE [*imitating a little girl*] Oh please, oh please, I want it, I've got to have it. Got to.

Stella takes a bunch of pins and starts to take the dress in. And as she does it she calls the measurements out to Gavin. We hold on Stella's movements, particularly the way she inserts the pins along Zee's bustline, and how each time we think she is going to stick it in Zee's flesh. The expression on Stella's face however is mischief more than malice.

STELLA [*loudly to Gavin*] Bust twenty-nine.

ZEE. Is that all? . . .

STELLA. Waist twenty-three-and-a-half, hips thirty-eight, shoulder to waist fourteen.

Zee slips out of the dress and puts on the first one which she selected, then takes a hat from the corner of the screen and dons it.

ZEE. Can I have my voile tomorrow? – I'm going away for a bit. I always go south in the winter. I need sun. I'm that kind of creature. What is it you can't do without?

Stella ignores the questions and calls through to Gavin:

STELLA. Can we have an alteration by tomorrow?

GAVIN. I suppose so.

Stella shrugs and Zee shrugs.

STELLA. What time do you need it by?

ZEE. I don't know, three, four.

STELLA. Let's say four.

ZEE. Send it by taxi. Do you have our address?

STELLA. No. You can put it on the back of the cheque.

ZEE. Oh, Stella . . . Can I have credit?

STELLA. I think we could risk that.

ZEE [*as she writes the address*] He's a bit thrifty but once he sees them and how they flow and that they're yours, he'll be charmed.

Zee hands the address to Stella.

ZEE. It's good you dressing me. It makes me feel like a little girl.

STELLA. But neither of us are that, are we?

They walk towards the door. Stella takes the hat off Zee.

STELLA. That's not for sale, that's mine.

Stella puts it on and Zee exits carrying the clothes she arrived in. Gavin appears in the doorway from the workroom.

GAVIN. So that's it, is it?

STELLA. That's her.

GAVIN. Ve-e-ry saucy.

STELLA. I couldn't let her have this hat, I'm too fond of it.

She puts it back on the screen. She lies on the couch for a moment, fanning herself with a newspaper, presaging her embattled future.

Chapter Five

Stella and her two sons, Oscar and Shaun, are laying a round table for dinner at home. The room is inviting, there are rosewood pieces, a religious tapestry, an open fire. It has an old-fashioned quality and contrasts with the Blakeley home which is pre-eminently modern. Oscar and Shaun are holding either handle of a silver tray, while Stella selects the cutlery, the glasses, the pepper and salt etc. At times either one of them pretends that he is going to let go of the tray. Stella's action of laying the table is continued over the speech.

OSCAR. If ever you get anything in your eye, you put salt water in it and then you close your eye and it makes it tear a lot and the thing comes out.

STELLA. Couldn't you just cry?

SHAUN. You mightn't be able to.

OSCAR. One of the boys in our dormitory cries at night and eats nuts. His parents are in Rio de Janeiro. I have to comfort him.

STELLA. How do you comfort him?

OSCAR. I say 'Pull yourself together, Cris' and

things like that. His name is Crispin but he's called Cris.

STELLA. You will talk, won't you. I mean after a while, after he's had a drink.

SHAUN and OSCAR [*together*] Of course.

STELLA. And listen. Take your time eating. We don't want everything devoured before he starts.

Stella takes some smoked salmon from the side, stuffs two big dollops into their mouths to keep them sated. Then she proceeds to decant some wine. She spills.

SHAUN. You're jittery.

OSCAR. What will we call him?

STELLA. Robert I suppose.

SHAUN. Or Bob. Hi, Bob.

That evening Stella, Robert, Shaun and Oscar are sitting at table, eating. The atmosphere is somewhat strained. They are eating asparagus and the children are dripping theirs. Stella is scarcely eating at all, anxious to make things smoother. She reaches over and wipes Oscar's chin with the end of her napkin.

ROBERT. Your mother's a good cook.

SHAUN. We know.

ROBERT. Do you like this school you're at?

SHAUN. It's all right.

ROBERT. I hated school. They used to call me Muggins. Muggins. But I got around that. I got this hamster, vicious, vicious teeth. [*Robert bares his teeth*]

I brought it everywhere, there was no Muggins after that. – I invented a whole town, drew it on paper. – I was always on the fringes of the Beasly gang, the Mitchell gang, the Flanagan gang ... [*Suddenly rises and grabs Shaun's lapel*] Listen, if you don't say something ...

OSCAR. I won't let you hit my bro ...

ROBERT [*grabbing the lapel tighter*] I'll hit your bro and I'll hit you ...

Oscar takes up a knife and brings it close to Robert's throat.

OSCAR. Touché.

Shaun takes up a knife. Shaun and Oscar charge him with knives. Robert takes up a knife too. Stella is perplexed, she is unable to remedy the situation.

The hall door is open and Stella is seeing Robert out. She gathers the collar of his coat up around his neck.

STELLA. Will you sleep?

ROBERT. I hope so.

STELLA. I had a dream about you. We got out of the car and you put money in a parking meter and it was on a slope.

ROBERT. That's significant.

STELLA. I don't know what possessed them, normally they're shy. – Will you forget it?

ROBERT. No.

Robert offers his hand with plasters on it, for her to kiss. She kisses it lightly and as he goes down the steps she closes the door. The two figures of Shaun and Oscar in pyjamas appear on the stairs.

SHAUN. We're sorry.

OSCAR. We're sorry.

Stella shakes her head but nevertheless goes towards them. As she sits on the stairs they unite in an embrace that is both tender and anguished. By their expressions they ask her forgiveness.

Chapter Six

Robert is in Zee's bedroom, looking at her clothes, her belongings. He holds the flame of a cigarette lighter near various objects of hers, her wigs, her evening dresses, her feather boa.

ROBERT [*an imaginary letter*] Dear Zee, Nice times seem to be impossible for us, it's all combat. Jabber, jabber. I'm tired of combat, dear Zee, I hope you are having a very good time. Stay away for as long as you like. I don't know what's happening to me, but something is . . .

Robert goes to his own room and starts to dress hurriedly. He puts on a white frilled shirt and is whistling ceaselessly to himself.

At the gambling casino Robert is standing at table playing dice. He is a little drunk. Each time as the dice is shaken he calls out persuasively.

ROBERT. Come on nine, come on nine.

But number 11 comes up.

ROBERT. Almost . . . almost.

As the chips are handed to the various winners

Robert crosses over to a cash desk and takes out a bundle of notes.

ROBERT. Give me a hundred in tens please.

By dawn Robert, another man and an elderly lady are all that's left. The lady is rolling the dice.

ROBERT. Come on nine, come on nine.

Number 4 comes up on the dice and they each smile regretfully. They each have lost. The two other players leave and Robert is last. Beside him is a champagne bottle in an ice bucket from which he has obviously been drinking. He combs his hair using the surface of the bucket as mirror. He picks the bottle out of the tub and considers how much is left. He drinks from the bottle. The croupier gets up and stretches and Robert hands him the bottle. As Robert leaves, a very pretty girl tries to catch his attention. He smiles at her, ruefully.

ROBERT. Sorry love, wrong time.

As he walks up the street, he helps himself to a bottle of milk from outside a café where there are crates of them.

Robert enters his own office. It is a private house really, with a tiny entrance hall and steep carpeted stairs. As he climbs the stairs he takes off the bow tie and unbuttons the shirt. Robert enters his own workroom. There are drawings everywhere hanging on the walls and great sheafs of them hanging on rods, in a long filing cabinet. He approaches his drawing desk on which there is a blank sheet of paper. He winces and goes to where there is an electric kettle, shakes it to see if there's water in it and glad that there is, plugs it in.

Chapter Seven

Late afternoon Robert is in a tee shirt and is spread-eagled over his drawing table, working. Various other drawings are on the floor all around him. They are the plans for offices, bathrooms, a refectory. Some are individual plans and some are the entire layout. There is an ashtray of hardly-smoked cigarettes next to him and a mug of tea which he has not touched. Rita, a young American girl with glasses and long hair, enters. She stands there, very timidly. She stands behind him looking at the drawing that he has done and the worship is apparent. The lens of one of her glasses is cracked. He appears to be oblivious of her at first.

ROBERT. Say whatever you've come to say.

RITA. Mrs Blakeley is downstairs.

Robert continues to add touches to his drawing.

RITA. Your wife is downstairs.

ROBERT. My wife, my lawnmower, my clients. [*Alert voice*] My wife is downstairs, why didn't you tell me?

RITA. You asked not to be disturbed.

Robert goes to a drawer in which there are various

pairs of dark spectacles. He selects a pair at random. He then starts to put on his dress shirt.

ROBERT. What time is it?

RITA. It's six thirty, she got here at four ten approximately.

ROBERT. Tell her I'm not here, tell her I've gone on a midnight dash, or to the races.

RITA. I've already told her you were working like crazy.

ROBERT. You bungle everything, don't you. Would you like to go and tell her you were misinformed?

RITA. No.

ROBERT. I thought you wouldn't. And do me a favour, will you? Those glasses, will you have them repaired. They get on my nerves, there's something so supplicating about them and you, you and your glasses, get a pair on the National Health.

Robert looks at his drawing, almost smiles and gives her a sort of biff as he leaves the room.

As he comes down the stairs his wife hurries up to meet him. She touches his dress shirt.

ZEE. Did you have a rotten day?

ROBERT. I had a very good day.

Robert ignores her touch and goes downstairs and she follows. As he goes out the door she grabs her suitcase and runs after him. In the street she has to run with the suitcase to keep up with him.

In the indoor carpark Robert hands the ticket and they wait in silence. When the attendant brings the car Zee jumps in. Robert doesn't. He goes to a small office, a glass booth really, to use the telephone. He dials without asking if he may. He hears it ringing at the other end and waits in vain for it to be answered.

In the car Zee has her person raised up from the seat to observe the proceedings. There is a barrage of horns blowing because the car is now holding up several others. Robert exits slowly from the booth and gets in and drives recklessly into the street.

ROBERT. Where can I drop you?

ZEE. Home! Home sweet home. – Aren't you going home? – I mean you don't have to come home specially because of me.

Robert is driving maniacally. Zee reaches over and takes off his glasses and starts to clean them with her dress.

ZEE. Something wrong somewhere. You've been working too hard. I always know when you've been working too hard. I can tell by the spot on your brow. It dries up. It's your little exhaustion zone, I haven't been sleeping either, awful people, all the same people but I thought they were awful without you, they need you, it needed you to give it any kind of, bouquet. I phoned you and they said they couldn't get an answer. I told them to keep trying but you know how they are, lazy, feckless, anyhow I'm back.

She puts the glasses on him.

ROBERT. They're worse.

ZEE. Yes, I know. I rubbed the grease in.

Robert leans over and opens the door to throw her

out but quickly she clambers over to the back of the car and gets down behind the seat.

ZEE. I'm not getting out, I'm not, you can have a situation if you like at the traffic lights but I refuse to get out and I'm tougher than you, far far tougher.

He drives murderously.

ZEE. That's right, kill us, let's die together as all true lovers do, let's die together.

At home Zee slings her suitcase along the floor in the direction of a cloakroom. Robert picks up letters from the floor and goes towards the telephone. Zee walks to the sitting-room. There is a small table laid for two. It is not the normal dining-room table, just a little occasional one which has been specially laid. The fire is set and a gas poker jutting from underneath. There is a very legible note propped up on the table. Zee goes towards the table.

ZEE. Intimate. A deux. How lovely. What are we having? Or should I say who are we having?

ZEE [*taking up the note and reading*] 'Dear Sir Robert' – who does she think she's writing to, *The Times*? – 'The joint will be ready at eight thirty. Hope everything is to your satisfaction. Yours truly, B. Donovan.'

Robert enters the room. He crosses to where glasses, bottles and ice bucket are on a tray. He pours himself a hefty drink.

ZEE. She hopes everything is to your satisfaction. B. Donovan. Quite a wit, our Mrs Thing when she puts pen to paper. One of the successors of Dean

Swift, villainous, I've always been warned off Irish people.

Zee busies herself about the room. She puts a match to the gas poker. She draws the curtains, making an incredible clatter. She hauls the gas poker out to light the candle on the table. Meanwhile Robert has sat down to look at his mail and has turned on a very harsh reading light.

ZEE. Don't. You'll destroy the illusion.

Robert looks at some of the envelopes and puts them in the fire without even opening them.

ZEE. Careful, one of them is from me. A billet doux. I let myself go. I often think people's letters are their true selves. Of course in the olden days people used to deliver them and wait for an answer under the casement.

Doorbell noise off.

ZEE. Ah.

Robert sits rigid, staring at a letter. Zee turns off the gas poker and uses her breath as a bellows for the fire. She uses the bellows itself to just puff back and forth in his direction.

Doorbell ring again.

Robert rises to answer it. Zee who has been crouching, rises too and jerks her hands agitatedly at him.

ZEE [*quietly*] Hey ... Robert, would you rather I left, made myself scarce?

ROBERT. Dean Swift.

Zee does a couple of quick body exercises to limber herself up. Stella enters in a long crimson dress, looking striking and full of composure. She is bearing a small gift, a little dish and with a certain sense of ceremony she walks towards Zee and hands it to her.

STELLA. Our first course.

It is covered with tinfoil which Zee rips away, then she smells it.

ZEE. Pâté, hurray! Did you make it yourself?

STELLA. Yes.

ZEE. Did you take quantities of belly of pork and veal and oddments from wild duck and pheasant, and dry white wine, and juniper berries and carcase and all that?

ROBERT. Zee, shut up.

ZEE [to Stella] That wasn't vicious was it?

STELLA. I cook to calm myself down.

ZEE. I holler. Would you like a martini? [To Robert] Would you like to mix the ladies a martini?

Robert goes over to the drinks area to do it and Zee draws Stella to the fire.

ZEE. You're cold.

STELLA. I couldn't get a taxi. They were all going home to their tea.

Robert shakes the martini mixer very vehemently and has already poured himself a second drink which he is downing.

ZEE. Pigs.

STELLA. He tried to charge me double, he thought I was a Norwegian.

ROBERT. Are you?

STELLA. What?

ROBERT. Norwegian.

STELLA. Of course not.

Robert walks towards them with two glasses ridiculously full. He is determined not to spill them. He makes a point of handing Stella hers first.

ZEE. She's a Celt, from the top of the morning country.

STELLA. I have Spanish blood.

ROBERT. And Spanish eyes.

Zee shrugs and makes some dismissing sound.

Zee and Stella sit opposite each other and Robert goes to the drinks place to replenish. Between Zee and Stella is a glass showcase, which is crammed with silver fishes.

ZEE. They're his silver fishes, his hobby, cold-blooded aquatic animals, breathing by means of gills, there's all sorts of fishes, puffer, swallower, whitefish, catfish, barracuda, walking fish, kissing fish, scavenger fish, flying fish.

ROBERT. Human fish.

ZEE. He loves the sea.

ROBERT. He has *never* said he loves the sea.

ZEE. Ha ha ha. One weekend we decided to be witty and do you know something – we were witty.

ROBERT. Yes, Mafia style.

ZEE. What did you do today? Some nice fittings?

STELLA [*ignoring the dig*] I had a lovely day. I didn't go near the shop, my sons were going back to school so we made toffee and we packed and we had our little weep. And I stood on the platform but they omitted to lean out of the window and wave.

ZEE. What ages are they?

STELLA. They're eleven, they're twins.

ZEE [*breathless*] Twins! [*Excited voice*] And did you breastfeed them? I met a man once, I sat next to him at dinner and he said you haven't lived until you see twins breastfed. He used to watch his wife. She used to lie on the bed, sprawled it seems, a tit in either direction.

Zee aims each of her breasts in opposite directions.

STELLA. I didn't have enough milk.

ZEE. Oh, you're like a dog I heard of, a Pyrenees sheepdog, had fourteen pups and only twelve tits, isn't nature cruel?

ROBERT. No, lamblike.

ZEE. I wish I'd met them, I like little girls and little boys, they always treat me as if I were one of them. My friend Jenny's little girls tell me everything. On the nanny's day out Jenny puts the clock on so that they can go to bed an hour earlier and they say the time always passes so quickly when we're with you, Mummy. And they're right, it does.

Zee looks up and sees no sign of Robert.

ZEE [*hollering*] Where are you?

Robert has gone behind the curtains.

STELLA. He's invisible.

Robert sticks his head out from between the curtains.

ROBERT [*to Zee*] Wouldn't you like to chew on

a teebone or a bit of gristle or something like that now?

ZEE [*rising*] Great, let's eat, let's eat out.

ROBERT. There's no going out, it's cooked.

ZEE [*holding two fingers up*] It's two fish, or two fowl, or two fillets or two something. And, we are three.

STELLA [*wryly*] You and I can eat small portions.

ZEE. Let him take us to a restaurant, at least there'll be other people to leaven the evening, to fill the gaps.

ROBERT. I haven't noticed any gaps. [*To Stella*] Have you?

STELLA [*with a smirk*] Chasms . . .

Zee exits, Robert walks closer to Stella.

ROBERT. Your dress is very beautiful, very becoming.

STELLA. It nearly always brings me bad luck though.

Robert places his hand palm down on her chest.

ROBERT. Your heart's steady.

STELLA [*indicating his shirt*] You're pretty snazzy yourself.

Zee re-enters, settling on her head a wide-brimmed hat that is exactly like the one she fitted on in Stella's shop. Robert makes a point of not moving his hand from Stella's chest for a beat. Zee makes another of her gestures of disdain. Robert and Stella go towards the door.

ZEE [*to Robert*] Darling. Don't you want to damp the fire down?

Robert turns and takes the ice-bucket, emptying

the contents, which is part ice, part water, on to the flames. Zee clicks out the light and quenches the candle, by blowing on it. In the darkness they each watch the flames subside.

ZEE. We have our little economies, you know.

The restaurant is full and noisy. They are at a table near a wall. Zee and Stella are on the inside. Behind them is a mirror. Robert has the choice of facing them or looking at himself in the mirror. He winces every time he sees himself. They each have enormous menus in their hands. There is a waiter at Robert's right. As Zee starts to talk Robert puts his hands to his ears.

ZEE [*to Stella*] This is our place, this is where we courted. They used to give us wine on the house. In those days it was not so chic, we made it so, didn't we? We had all our correspondence addressed here. One lunchtime I found a pearl in my oyster, a grotty little pearl but still, a pearl.

Zee suddenly turns her attention to the waiter, beams at him, greets him in husky Italian.

ZEE. *Ah, Signore, buona sera. Come sta? Bene, benissimo.* [*To Stella*] He comes from Parma, where the violets grow.

ROBERT [*to Stella*] The lads went back today?

STELLA. Unfortunately.

ZEE. I bet neither of you two know about Parma violets.

ROBERT. Even if we did we wouldn't deprive you of the pleasure of telling us.

ZEE [*to Stella*] Well, they're very delicate and they cost a fortune. And they're what people give when they want to give something really special, when they're in love, or someone dies, or something out of the ordinary.

Robert gestures to Stella for the waiter to take her order.

STELLA. Melon and dover sole.

ROBERT [*as he smiles at her*] The same.

WAITER. That's all, sir?

ROBERT. That's all.

ZEE [*rubbing her hands*] Well that's not very celebratory, let's see, I'll have pasta, *spaghetti al dente*, then I'll have some duck, *canard*.

The waiter gathers the menus and turns away.

ZEE. Hey, you can bring the *vino* now. Pronto.

Robert starts drawing with a stylo on a white napkin, he is drawing a plan of a house, then he unfolds the napkin and continues to draw.

ZEE. Yes, we were witty, the first witticism came from him. He wakened up, he said can we do something really erotic today, eroticer than we did yesterday.

Chapter Eight

Robert enters his office, clicks on the light. In his head he can quite clearly hear Zee's voice: 'You haven't lived until you've seen twins breastfed. She used to lie on the bed, sprawled it seems, a tit in either direction, she used to lie on the bed, sprawled in either direction, she used to lie on the bed . . .' He removes his jacket and from the pocket takes the napkin on which he has been drawing. He rolls up his sleeves and goes towards the drawing board. He takes the existing drawing off the board and discards it. He sellotapes a clean sheet of white paper on to the board. He starts to draw, then remembers something. He walks across to the telephone, picks up the receiver, puts it in his coat, making a little nest for it. Now he is hearing Zee's voice at different speeds as if it were a record which was put on at the wrong speed, so that it went squa, squa, squa. The voice takes up speed.

Chapter Nine

Stella and Zee are still at the restaurant table. The waiter is standing over them.

WAITER. He just said Good night, buona notte...

ZEE. I think he's getting an ulcer.

WAITER. Could be. Everyone has an ulcer these days.

ZEE. Except me.

Waiter walks away and Zee hits the table a couple of bangs. Stella settles herself.

ZEE. Are you broken-hearted?

STELLA. Not particularly.

ZEE [*laughing*] Yes you are. You feel that he's let you down.

STELLA. *Et tu, Brute.*

ZEE. I'm used to it. I'm tough. – Do you want to have a good cry?

STELLA. I want the supper, the nosh.

ZEE. 'Atta girl.

Waiter places the melon in front of Stella and spaghetti in front of Zee. Zee takes a dish of grated cheese, tumbles it over the spaghetti. They commence to eat. Zee makes an appreciative sound while still chewing.

STELLA. My husband isn't in the country, he's dead.

ZEE. I know.

STELLA. Why didn't you say so?

ZEE. I didn't want to put you in a spot. And anyhow you ran out of the room to cry or throw up or something.

Zee twirls some spaghetti on her fork and gives a mouthful to Stella.

ZEE. So you're on the loose?

Stella has to swallow before answering. She levers her hand from left to right, indicating yes-and-no.

STELLA. Not exactly.

They both continue to eat from their respective plates.

ZEE. I think you've got the best of both worlds.

The mood between them is much more relaxed and Stella is definitely smiling.

ZEE. If we were at school together would we have been friends?

STELLA. On and off.

ZEE. You would have been prefect.

STELLA. I might not. Yes, I do feel that he let us down, that he's a rat and a louse and that he has no b . . . backbone and that if he can't cope with a situation he oughtn't to let himself in for it, or you, or me.

ZEE [*patting her hand*] I'll get him to send you some Parma violets tomorrow.

STELLA. I got expelled at school.

49

ZEE. So did I! What did you do wrong?

STELLA. What did you do?

ZEE. No you.

STELLA. No you.

ZEE. No you.

The waiter is standing holding a bottle of wine for the label to be inspected and is amused by their conviviality. He winks at another waiter to take cognizance of it all.

Chapter Ten

In her shop Stella is engaged in fitting a capacious gown on a young girl. Robert enters quietly and stands to observe. He is smiling. Gavin puts down his coffee mug, approaches him with a beam.

GAVIN. Can I help you, sir?

ROBERT. No, I'm waiting for –

Robert indicates Stella.

GAVIN. Oh, for Madam.

Stella turns and sees Robert and rises from her knees. She has a bunch of pins in her mouth. She excuses herself to the young girl and crosses to where Robert is. He takes the pins from her mouth.

ROBERT. Nice place you've got here. – A touch of the Orient . . .

Stella glares at him.

ROBERT. Can I talk to you, somewhere?

He indicates the small room.

STELLA. That's a fitting room.

ROBERT [*smiling*] This is a fitting room.

STELLA. You can see I'm busy.

ROBERT. I couldn't carry it off, I wasn't equal to it.

STELLA. Apparently.

ROBERT. I didn't know she was coming back. She appeared in my office.

STELLA. You're both great at appearing.

ROBERT. I worked all night.

STELLA. Glad you got some inspiration.

ROBERT. You think I have no backbone don't you?

STELLA. I don't think anything much.

ROBERT. Let's have dinner tonight. You can bawl me out.

STELLA. Why should I. It's your little inferno and it's all very boring and brittle and trite.

ROBERT. God, you're astringent.

STELLA. No, just superior.

Stella rejoins her customer who has been watching, along with Gavin.

Robert hesitates for a minute, then leaves.

Stella kneels down once again and starts to turn up the hem. She is very close to tears. Gavin gives her a sip from his coffee mug.

That night Stella, wearing a housecoat, comes through the hall to answer the door. She opens it and there is Robert. He stretches his hand out to make a declamatory gesture.

ROBERT. I come to you with all my backbone. [*He puts his hand to his forehead, having decided that he has made the wrong speech*] No. [*Another gesture*] I come to you with all my shadows. No. [*A third gesture*] I come to you as an inferior.

STELLA. I've got somebody here.

ROBERT [*a little taken aback*] A man?

He looks at her and guesses that she has lied. He immediately decides to comply with the lie.

He enters the house, and taking a carving knife from the kitchen and one of Stella's boots as weapons to hand, he runs from one room to the other and then up the stairs.

ROBERT. Where is he?

> Out damned lover, out I say.
>
> What's his build?
>
> Let me at him.
>
> Is he square shouldered?
>
> Is he a cricket or a soccer fan?
>
> What's his handicap?

As he goes from room to room. Stella follows him and finally catches up with him in her bedroom. She is laughing now and as she comes towards him he knots the bow of her dressing gown.

ROBERT. There's something I haven't told you about, a problem, I never know what to do about it, I wonder if I can confide.

STELLA. Tush-tush.

ROBERT [*banging his pocket*] Small change.

Stella takes the various coins from his pockets and goes to the mantelpiece and arranges them in small banks. Robert stands behind her, kissing her all the while.

Robert gets out of his car and closes the door very quietly. He enters his own house but does not turn on the light. He flicks on his lighter to guide his way to the first step of the stairs. He quenches the lighter. His shoes creak. He takes off one shoe and then the other. There is utter quiet. He enters his own bedroom and closes the door, relieved.

Chapter Eleven

Next morning Robert is in bed asleep when Zee enters carrying an enormous breakfast tray and is full of gusto. She places the breakfast tray on a bedside table and draws the curtains.

ZEE. Fresh grapefruit segments, fried herrings in oatmeal with grilled Ayrshire bacon, toast, hot soft rolls or muffins with butter and marmalade, tea or coffee.

Robert sits up in bed, sees the tray of food, winces.

ZEE. I got it out of the paper – suggestions for the day. It's nice to be domesticated.

ROBERT. Now and then.

Zee hands him a plate of food and the morning paper. Robert takes the paper but not the food. She pours him a cup of coffee which he does accept. He opens the paper and begins to read it, she sits on the bed and opens a paper, the same one as his, a *Times*. She is humming to herself.

ZEE. How do you feel about a theatre?

Robert looks to see if she is reading the same paper and is exasperated to find she is.

ZEE. Well you always want it when I want it.

ROBERT. I never heard such extravagance in all my life.

ZEE. How do you feel about a theatre?

ROBERT. I don't.

ZEE. You can't be with her every night. You'll wear each other out.

ROBERT. It's only wearing when it's something you don't want to do, when it goes against the grain. Didn't you know that?

Zee tops an egg with a cut of a knife and then dips a spoon in it for him.

ZEE. Is it very genial? Do you watch her make a fruit salad? I assume she can cook. That would be one of her trump cards. And I bet she's got a footstool. I always know the kind of cow who has a footstool.

ROBERT. She suggests you open a fish stall.

ZEE [laughing] I can just see it. You stretched on a goatskin, invoking childhood memories, your poverty, your traumas, the way you never saw your mother because she had to scrub ... of course she's a good listener, everyone's a good listener at first. Then very soon you get her little cantata, alone, not understood and good, too good. It's a little bit archaic you know.

Robert gets out of bed and goes to the bathroom. She follows.

ROBERT. And who are you? Miss Rheingold with the rasp and the cigarette holder. It's a bit archaic you know.

ZEE. I bet the pair of you wail. You ought to make a record.

ROBERT. We make lots of things.

ZEE. Hu-hu, the fertility man, speaking.

ROBERT. To his hag.

Robert starts to shave.

ZEE. You're in a muddle. You don't know who loves you, there's her and there's all those little adoring apprentices with their hair and their boobs and their crushes [*Blowing the shaving lather over his face*] and there's me.

ROBERT. Frothing?

Robert dislodges the lather from the end of the blade, strewing it in different directions.

ZEE. You're in your prime. – Hold your stomach in.

ROBERT. Why don't you take a lover?

ZEE. Is that what you recommend?

ROBERT. He can put the meals down to me and the theatre tickets and whatever other expenses he incurs.

Zee touches him with the end of her necklace on the navel, as if it were a stethoscope she was using.

ZEE. But remember how jealous you are, it's like an alarm inside you, you go mad, you start ringing people, you go through my things, and then you get all your white spots and they don't enhance you, do they? Only last week when I came in that hire car to that function and you were waiting for me on the steps, you got very hot and bothered 'cos I'd been sitting next to the driver and because I took a moment to get out, you thought the worst. You thought we were finishing something off, you had to have me, there and then in a lane. [*Sings*] – South of the Border,

57

Down an old rusty lane . . . down Mexico way.

Robert throws her out and closes the door.

ROBERT. Slut!

ZEE [*with her hand on the bathroom door*] But that's part of it. That's why you're still here. You like the tussle. You like the uncertainty. You don't know what I did yesterday, you don't know who I saw and what went on, you don't know what I'll do today. Nor do I.

ROBERT. Enjoy yourself.

ZEE. I had a thing in Spain, with a doctor. I like doctors. They have a secret, the Midas touch. He said, 'Shall I undress you like a doctor?' He was very good-looking, very hardworking, six children, busy; the waiting-room was full of people, we could hear them on the other side, we had to whisper, he panted.

Robert opens the door and with the razor in one hand brings his face very close to hers.

ROBERT. And?

ZEE. I'm not going to be the cause of your white spots again . . .

Robert crosses to the bedroom. She follows and puts some of the boiled egg on the spoon and goes towards him to give him some.

ROBERT. You lay with him on the floor, didn't you. Or maybe it was the couch, the good old utility couch, with people on the other side, unfortunate people, and you gave him one of your quick jabs, you swept the unfortunate man off his feet, thank God you can't conceive or I'd be maintaining a reformatory. You always get them like that, quick, bang, before they know where they are, a punch in the face, a whiff of ammonia, but you don't keep them, you can't keep them, you cannot keep the love of a man.

ZEE. I'm keeping you.

ROBERT. No you're not, baby.

He throws the spoon of egg in her face. He takes his jacket and goes.

As Zee hears the hall door bang she lies on his bed and buries her face on the pillow, at the same time thumping it. Then she sees the breakfast tray and starts to squash bits of food into useless pieces.

When Robert enters the house that evening Zee is dressed in riding gear. She is standing before the mirrors and on the table underneath is a riding cap and whip. Robert takes up the whip.

ROBERT. And where do you think you're going?

ZEE. Riding. Horsey horsey. Boggie-woggie. Funny lot there. A man brings roses with ribbon round them. A lord. Says his house is ghastly, like a laundry, [*Smiling*] his roses are nice though, they smell.

ROBERT. You have a gala time.

ZEE. I always have a gala time. [*Abstractedly; and to herself in the mirror*] Now let's see if I've got everything.

Zee takes up the whip, puts on the riding cap, touches her breasts, her crotch, either thigh, and pretends to be unaware of his reaction which is that of mounting fury. He retrieves the whip and with the other hand clutches her by the throat. Her astonishment manifests itself in a smile.

ROBERT. We're going to go over our bills, settle our accounts, before everything is cut off, heat, light, phone, sewerage.

ZEE. Bills will lead to a quarrel, argie-bargie.

ROBERT. That's what we arranged to do. That's why I came straight home.

ZEE. We can do these some morning. [*Taking her diary and pencil*] Let's make a date.

ROBERT. No, we can't.

He snatches the diary, takes the hat and puts it on his own head, but back to front. He hits the table with the whip.

ZEE. You're hitting the table.

ROBERT. Would you rather I hit you?

ZEE. Poor baby, in a sulk. I don't want you to give up an evening, I mean they're so love-laden, they're so precious, all that footstool bit.

ROBERT. The housekeeping is overdrawn, I know when it's overdrawn, you start buying things, getting lavish, fried herrings, Ayrshire bacon.

ZEE. Wait till she finds out that you're a miser. Because if I'm any judge she's a bit of a one for the consumer goods herself.

Zee makes a move for the door. Robert grabs her shoulders and stands in her way.

ROBERT. You can reconcile yourself to the fact that you're not going.

zee. That cap suits you. I might give it to you if you play your cards right.

Robert is baulked for a moment, lets go of her shoulders.

robert. This Lord so-and-so, it's not the season for roses.

zee. Roses, snapdragons, what's the difference. [*She tries to go to the door*] They'll be waiting.

robert. They can wait. The chinless wonders. Lords, loafers.

She escapes but he takes hold of her hands and insists they have a fist fight. She makes sounds to spur him on, as if she were a mere spectator.

zee. Don't tell me you're getting jealous all over again.

robert. No, just practical. It's what I planned to do, and it's what I'm going to do.

He turns her round, takes hold of both her hands and marches her towards the study. She is a little recalcitrant but it is to sustain the tension.

zee. It's like gym or something.

Robert clicks on the light in the study and closes the door firmly. He leads her across to a chair and with the whip binds her hands to the chair. She hices up and down like a little girl and screams, gustily.

zee. It's not fair. It's not proper. I'm prisoner. You can't keep me here. I'll shout. I'll expose you. The neighbours will come in. The clean-living diplomats will come in, let me out, let me out, let me out.

Robert holds a cushion to her face so that her screams are muffled. She screams for a bit, then he removes the cushion and she starts up again.

ZEE. Woman-hater. Jew-hater. Swine. Imperialist!

He replaces the cushion again, and she does a very high scream that she gradually brings down lower and lower. There is silence.

ROBERT. Finished?

She nods and exhales to show that she is out of breath. Robert drops the cushion on her lap. He goes to a drawer in the filing cabinet and lifts out the whole drawer, which is stuffed with bills, envelopes, forms, numerous photos of Zee. He empties the contents on to the desk, clicks on another table lamp and sits down opposite her.

ZEE. There's roses for every season of the year and also strawberries. That's part of my gardening lore.

He lights a cigarette. She whistles softly to alert his attention. He is reading one of the documents. She whistles again. He looks up.

ZEE [in a Cockney accent] Officer givvus a drag.

Robert hands it to her but her hands are bound. She leans forward and he places it between her lips. She draws on the cigarette deeply and pleasurably. Still holding it in her mouth she stretches back and raises her chair so that the front legs are off the ground. At the same time she stretches her legs forward. He snaps his fingers, indicating that he wants the cigarette back. She doesn't budge. She smiles. He comes round to her side of the desk and takes the cigarette from between her lips. She closes her mouth

62

but tilts it towards him in a grimace. Her legs are fully stretched and the cushion slides off her lap. She opens her legs.

ZEE. You're gorgeous.

He hesitates for a moment, then turns on his heels and walks out of the room. She immediately rises in anger, forgets that she is bound, and vehemently and with the certainty of success, she begins with her shoulders and arms to tug at the rope and loosen the knot.

It is late when Robert returns. He enters his own house but does not turn on the light: instead he flicks on his lighter to guide his way to the first step of the stairs. He quenches the lighter. He takes off one shoe and then the other. As he climbs the stairs a blaze of light is turned on on the top landing and Zee appears in a very fetching short nightdress.

ZEE. Not bad. I thought you would have stayed till morning. It's most unfeeling of you, it's what a woman craves most, still it's an ill wind. Does she come or does she fake it or would you know?

Robert goes towards the bathroom.

ZEE. Ah! You didn't bathe there? You didn't feel ready to? You didn't have your own set of towels? I know the feeling.

Robert goes into the bathroom, closes the door and locks it.

ZEE. I'm in blue. Something old, something new, something borrowed and something blue.

In the bathroom Robert is hauling linen, pillows, out of a hot press and is making up a bed in the bath. Zee is looking through the keyhole. She looks with one eye, then the other, then she talks through the keyhole.

ZEE. What are you up to? What pranks are you up to? Are you weighing yourself? Robert. Roberto. Bobby. Bob. I'm in blue.

Robert steps into his bath bed. The first drawback is that the tap isn't fully turned off. He lies so that his feet are at the tap end. He positions himself in different ways. Zee gets up and goes to her own room, pulls a blanket from her bed, calls out 'Good night' giving the impression that she has gone to bed and then steals back on to the landing. She settles down on the floor to one side of the bathroom door. Robert rises, steps out of the bath and, with a sheet round him, opens the door carefully and gleefully, sees no sign of her, steps out. As he does, she catches hold of his ankle, then the calf of his other leg, then the back of his knee. Then she draws him down towards her and as she does, pulls her nightdress up over her face. Robert is surprised but not resistant.

ZEE. You'll always have women all over you, because you know how to treat them, you use them and you abuse them and you make them suffer, I don't resent it, as for her she's nothing, she just whets my appetite. I'll fight her a duel any day, and win.

Zee covers them both with the sheet and purrs with delight.

Chapter Twelve

Some evenings later Robert and Stella enter their favourite restaurant. Stella goes to the ladies room. Robert sits at the small cocktail bar. The waiter gives him a nod and Robert returns the nod and retreats to the hall immediately. As Stella walks towards him he turns her round, to face the main door.

ROBERT. A friend of ours is there.

STELLA. No! With who? With whom?

ROBERT. One of her lackeys, no doubt.

STELLA. But how did she know we were coming?

ROBERT. She must have rung and found out I'd booked a table.

STELLA. God what a nerve.

ROBERT. We'll have to find a new place.

STELLA. Or you'll have to train her to behave herself.

Zee and Aubrey, a young boy of about twenty, are sitting at table, eating. They are both slightly drunk.

AUBREY. Do it to him, dear, have an affair with some gorgeous man.

ZEE. If your lot don't stop increasing and multiplying there'll be no one to do it with. After females I hate your lot next, your mincey-incey lot.

AUBREY. No need to get personal, dear. Or I won't do your hair nice next time. What's she like?

ZEE. A slob, and even worse than that, a soulful slob. There is nothing I hate more than soulful people, she's always a little out of breath, and she sees beauty in everything, specially in shit.

AUBREY. Good figure?

ZEE. Awful. Pendulous breasts and all that.

AUBREY. Nom-nom, I wouldn't mind a drop.

ZEE. You wouldn't know a wet mother if you saw one.

AUBREY. I would, I'm a very good judge, despite my . . . tendencies.

ZEE. Do you think I've got good breasts?

AUBREY. Super.

ZEE. You're a liar, I've got none. I've got foam-rubber. Do you want to feel it?

Zee is adjusting her false breast, and he is trying to restrain her.

AUBREY. Later dear, later. – What does Zee want naughty boy to do?

ZEE. There's a geezer who works for her. One of the madam syndrome shit, and I want you to chat him up.

AUBREY. I'd be found out straight away.

ZEE. No you won't because I'll brief you.

AUBREY. Ah me . . . a plot.

ZEE. I'll make you a present of one of her robes,

you love her things, I know you love her things.

AUBREY. They're divine things, absolutely divine.

ZEE. And I might even give you a shirt to go with it. And a couple of silk scarves to catch the boys.

AUBREY. Well, what do you want me to find out?

ZEE. Everything, their movements, her movements, I have a hunch they're going somewhere, he's been dropping dark hints about a business trip. This Gavin will know.

AUBREY. I can't ask him straight out.

ZEE. No, but you can wangle your way into their lives.

AUBREY. I never felt such a rat.

ZEE. It's time you did.

AUBREY. You are a bitch.

ZEE. Yes, I'm a bitch. Open. Straight. There's plenty of fellows, there's plenty around, she can have anyone she likes but not him. Also, try and be her hairdresser. Shave her head.

AUBREY. But it isn't as if you'd both been angels.

ZEE. This is different, he actually cares for her, they write each other letters. She refuses to have lunch with him because she likes to brood. I nearly ran her over the other day. She was in a square, staring at mother nature. I trailed her. She was so full of her fucking meditation that she didn't even see me. Fine one she'd be in the jungle. He gave her a ring.

AUBREY. Oh, what kind?

ZEE. Just an ordinary ring, not an engagement ring or anything like that. Just an expensive ring.

AUBREY. Wonder he didn't give her a bracelet.

Zee calls over to the waiter.

ZEE. My husband not arrive yet?

WAITER. No, madam.

The waiter goes away and Zee leans over to Aubrey.

ZEE. Let's put a few curses on her, let's hope they're crashing and he escapes by the skin of his teeth and she's disfigured. I don't want to give her the satisfaction of being dead. And her kids, let's put a little affliction on them.

AUBREY. Zee, I refuse to sit with you, I refuse to have innocent children victimized.

ZEE. Oh, paternoster! [*In a softer voice*] You will do it, won't you? I mean, you'll go there and have a look, browse.

AUBREY. I'll have to think it over.

ZEE. You'll go there and select the robe you want me to buy for you and chat him up. Tit for tat. He gave her an amethyst.

AUBREY. That must be her birthstone.

ZEE. I go through his pockets in the middle of the night. If she ever has to hock it, it won't take her very far.

AUBREY. I could do with some new clothes. Haven't told you what happened to me, dear, went to the club the other night, having a quiet gin and tonic all on my ownie, I'd had my supper, one of those ghastly meals in a minute things, and this divine creature prances over, and he had the evening paper and he had it rolled up and he gives me a biff with it and says, 'Why are you drinking gin, you know it's bad for your liver,' bought me a brandy, brandy kills me, makes my heart go poom poom poom, gave me another supper, divine table manners, had a delicious recipe for strawberry mousse, adds champagne to it, got me all steamed up, said it was as long as the evening paper, nearly died I did, went scarlet 'fraid somebody would overhear. So I brought it home, and we had a boozy time and a boozy sleep and I get up in the morning, and it's gone. And all my records and my Regency shirt and my leather jerkin, you know my leather jerkin. And that gorgeous Victoriana suit that you like. All my best things. Only my best things.

ZEE [*rising*] Let's go and knock 'em up.

Outside Stella's house Zee drives up on to the pavement and brings the car to a screaming standstill. The house is in darkness except for a dim light upstairs. Zee winds the window down and hollers:

ZEE. At it no doubt, à la candlelight, sacramental valley.

AUBREY. If you think I'm getting out of this car you're mistaken.

ZEE. You yellow bastard, you buff bastard.

Zee gets out and enters the gateway. Inside the gate is a dustbin which she drags along the path making a dreadful din and as she gets to the doorstep she empties the contents. Immediately she runs back towards her car. A second and stronger light is turned on in Stella's house.

Robert and Stella are in bed. The clatter of the dustbin lid brings them to. Robert rises and goes to the window and just catches sight of Zee's car driving off.

ROBERT. Oh, some rowdies . . .

Stella rises at once to look. Robert draws the curtains close and stands there not allowing her to open them. She tugs at one.

STELLA. Your wife, your darling wife.

Stella nips in underneath the curtain and, leaning on the windowsill, looks down to her front path, seeing the shambles.

ROBERT. Oh, it's just kid stuff.

STELLA. You idiot . . . can't you see.

Robert stays outside the curtains and Stella is on the inside. They confront each other by talking through a parting in the curtain as if one or other were on a stage.

STELLA. She's possessed.

ROBERT. She's a silly woman.

STELLA. Who would do anything. Kill me, my kids . . .

ROBERT. You're getting carried away.

STELLA. What if I told you that she followed me the other day, in her car, your car, tried to run me over.

ROBERT [*disturbed*] You should have run her over.

STELLA. I was on foot.

ROBERT. We'll have her certified.

STELLA. I do love your company and all that, but I didn't reckon for her and she's too much, she's everywhere.

ROBERT [*opening the curtain in order to be near her*] She's not here.

STELLA. I can't sleep, I can't eat, the shop is going to pieces, I haven't done anything for my collection, the fabrics aren't ordered . . .

ROBERT. I'll have to take more care of you . . . I will have to . . .

STELLA. I have the most terrible omens . . .

ROBERT. That I'm going to take you away, to the sun.

STELLA. I'm not an invalid.

ROBERT. To the sea then, the wild and wintry . . . and it's going to be a top secret and you're going to forget all about your shop and your collections and my wife and . . .

STELLA. I wonder which of us has the least sense, you or I.

They sit and embrace on the window sill, forgetting that the bed is near.

Chapter Thirteen

The following evening Robert enters the house in a great fluster. He is about to go straight up the stairs when Zee comes from the kitchen area and calls to him.

ZEE. Take it easy, Romeo. – There's some hitch. – Something to do with one of her kids.

Robert comes back downstairs.

ROBERT. What, what?

ZEE. I don't know, she didn't elaborate.

ROBERT. Where is she?

ZEE. She's on her way there, and she's going to ring you from a callbox.

Zee takes his hand and brings him into the sitting-room.

ZEE. Let's have a little drinkies.

Robert sits down and Zee pours an ordinary drink for herself and a very stiff one for him. Zee sits near him on a pouffe.

ZEE. Well, cheers. – I suppose she felt a bit awkward ringing me.

ROBERT. Which of her kids is it?

ZEE. I don't know, one or the other. She sounded desperate.

ROBERT. Was she going there alone?

ZEE. She was going to some hospital.

ROBERT. Is it that bad?

ZEE. Seemingly – So you'll be a bit late getting away.

ROBERT. She idolizes those kids.

ZEE. Does she have a favourite?

ROBERT. No, but she's nicer to Oscar because he's shy.

ZEE. Does he suffer from an inferiority complex?

ROBERT. I think so. His brother is a bit of a bomb . . . and gets away with it.

ZEE. God, I'd hate that, I never had a sister, thank God, I mean you and your brothers, you're all very palsy-walsy when you meet for Christmas and reunions, but there is a wedge, isn't there?

ROBERT. There was. I thought up methods of poisoning my brothers, putting a little pinch in the porridge.

ZEE. Strychnine . . . ?

ROBERT. Yeh. We used to have it for foxes.

Zee touches his knee.

ZEE. It's tough on you, this. The funny thing is anything you look forward to never happens.

ROBERT. That's nothing, but if *she's* in trouble . . .

ZEE. Still, it was going to be lovely, idyllic.

She brings the bottle and pours him another drink. Robert tries to intercept her, but nicely.

ROBERT. No, no, no. I don't want to get drunk.

ZEE. Will I make you a sandwich? Or give you a neck rub?

Zee puts her drink down, stands behind him and starts slowly and concentratedly to rub his neck. She says the same words over and over again, soft, hypnotic, murmurous.

ZEE. Give it to me, give it to me, give me your neck, it's my neck now, it's not your neck any more, and I'm making it all lovely and liquid, and loose and languorous, it's like a river your neck, flowing . . .

Robert closes his eyes for a moment and then sits up suddenly.

ROBERT. Gavin would know where she is.

ZEE [*a little too hastily*] No he wouldn't, they rang her at home.

ROBERT. When did she say she'd phone?

ZEE. She didn't, she just said you're to wait here, to sit tight until she phones you.

With his shoulders he flings her hands away, and rises. He goes towards the door.

ROBERT. You'll have your blood shed yet. I'll see to that if God doesn't.

ZEE. You . . . bastard.

She throws his glass and then starts to break things to hand, in the room.

Chapter Fourteen

Stella is standing waiting by the barrier at the railway station. She is looking anxious as the train is about to go. People are milling by in all directions. Robert appears from an unexpected direction with the tickets in his mouth. They go through the barrier and run for it.

ROBERT. Darling, you're mad, I wouldn't let you down. I'd never let you down, you know that.

He turns to see her reaction but she is now crying.

ROBERT. There was a little hitch. There was an attempt to detain me but I foiled it.

STELLA [*harshly*] Why don't you say her?

ROBERT. Her.

They jump on to the moving train.

ROBERT [*exultant*] Dracula, Draculae, Draculas, Dracularum, Draculis, Draculis.

They enter a first-class sleeper. It is cosy and welcoming. First thing, he takes a bottle of whisky from his bag and offers some to her. She hesitates for a second, he brings the bottle to her lips. She declines. He pours some into the metal stopper and gives it to her like a medicine.

Chapter Fifteen

Zee is climbing the dingy stairs of a brothel, taking money out of her big bag. Entering the ante-room she passes some notes to an elderly woman who is sitting, knitting.

ZEE. How much?

The woman takes the required number of notes and points to a door.

ZEE. And do I have a choice?

The woman continues to point to the door and Zee enters it by kicking. Inside is a good-looking young boy who is much too tall for her. She looks up at him.

ZEE. Don't talk to me. Don't tell me you loved your cousin or any crap like that.

Zee starts to pull off his clothes.

BOY. That is what I am supposed to do to you.

ZEE. Except that I'm better at it.

Suddenly she loses heart.

ZEE. Oh shit. Let's have a drink.

She turns away from him.

BOY. You want. You don't want?

She sits on the bed and moves agitatedly to make

the mattress squeak to give the illusion that they are in the throes of love-making.

ZEE. Pretty boy.

BOY. You don't want.

Zee puts her finger to her lips to stop him talking. She shakes her head and puts out her hand for him to forgive. He shakes it limply and goes to the window and looks out, bored. She starts to tie her buttons etc. and in doing so she laughs loudly, simulating the laughter of joy. He turns and looks at her as if she has gone mad. She goes on laughing.

Chapter Sixteen

Robert and Stella climb a steep path that leads towards a small cottage. They are laden with packages, groceries etc. Stella is walking a bit behind, looking round, happy, breathing deeply. The cottage lies ahead, and around are the mountains and the scrubland. The Scottish countryside is clear, clean and spacious after where they have come from.

STELLA. You are clever.

ROBERT. You like it.

STELLA. I love it. – I'm in my element.

ROBERT. What is your element?

STELLA [*puffing a bit because of the climb*] Tell you later . . .

They walk on.

ROBERT. All we need now is a sheepdog.

STELLA. And wood smoke.

They enter the cottage by a lych gate. Robert puts down the bags, but piles some groceries and a carrier containing wine bottles, on to Stella, while he looks for the key. He feels under a big stone, then lifts another stone, then puts his hand above the lintel.

ROBERT. Now where did he say?

STELLA [*mock panic*] They're slipping, they're slipping . . .

ROBERT. Hold on.

Robert finds the key at last, but deaf to her protestations opens the door slowly and leisurely. The mood between them is only gay.

They enter the kitchen and while she dumps the various things on the table he crosses to feel the stove which is cold. He lifts the top up. She takes off her coat and rubs her hands with cold. He takes a sweater from his bag and puts it on her. She then takes an apron which is hanging from a nail and puts that on. They busy themselves making it warm and habitable.

Robert chops up some wood, taking great pleasure in doing it, chopping the pieces very finely, pleased with his skill.

Stella goes from the kitchen to the living-room, exploring, and then the bedroom. She runs across and wipes the window to see out. She sees the mountains. She runs and does the same to the other window and sees more mountains and likes it exceedingly.

Stella is by the table, cutting scones that she has just made when Robert enters with logs.

ROBERT. Ours . . . all ours.

He deposits the logs and watches her as she cuts the scones.

ROBERT. What would you like first . . . sons or daughters?

STELLA. Both.

ROBERT. You shall have them. Both.

Stella arranges the scones on a floured tray.

The next evening Stella is lying on a rug in front of the fire while Robert is applying a suntan lotion to her back and legs. He reads the instructions aloud.

ROBERT. This great adventure in tanning without sun, you can obtain a glorious Med. tan in your own home. Because it is a creamy mousse . . .

Stella touches various parts of her back which she feels he has ignored.

ROBERT. They'll think you're Eurasian.

STELLA. Would you like if I was?

ROBERT. Don't be ridiculous.

STELLA. I'm not really your type.

ROBERT. You are now.

STELLA. But I wasn't.

ROBERT. I like all types. I used to like prostitutes – they talk less. I had this dream, this vision, whole streets of whores under street lights. They were where I went in my formative years.

STELLA. You mean you had no girlfriend?

ROBERT. Not many. I didn't know what to say to them.

STELLA. And then Zee came along. Did you court her properly?

ROBERT. Court her? I was dragged into it, she had a letter of introduction to me from a friend of mine in

Africa. He and I were students together and he asked me to see that she was alright, she appeared with a lilo.

STELLA. But you didn't turn her away.

ROBERT. I was sharing a flat with a couple of others. She was young then and she didn't talk so much. She had this bicycle, she used to go all over London on a bicycle. She went a lot to the Zoo. She cooked a bit for us. She wasn't my girl in particular, she was anyone's.

Stella rises and looks in the mirror, at her tan.

STELLA. People never want to admit they were in love once it's over.

ROBERT. I'm forgetful, I forget.

STELLA. The times you sat on a bench and waited, or danced a foxtrot or went for a walk in the frost and hawed on someone's fingers.

ROBERT. Ah, now, you're talking about something real.

STELLA. There are so many things that I would like to know about you.

ROBERT. Ditto.

STELLA. What goes on in that noddle?

ROBERT. Oh ... cranes, concrete, ceilings, you and me, us, the situation.

Stella is measuring herself with a tape.

STELLA. I've put on half an inch ...

ROBERT. I don't like to ask you this, but, I've often thought about it. Am I like him? I mean, do I bear any resemblance to him?

STELLA. Who?

ROBERT. Your . . . husband.

STELLA [*tersely*] No.

ROBERT. Pity.

The telephone rings and they both jump. Robert picks up the phone and to assist things Stella clicks on a light which destroys the candlelight gentleness of the room.

Stella looks at Robert as he holds the receiver, but he gives her no clue, looks away, then turns his back on her.

ROBERT. Yes, it is me. What's happened? What's wrong? Well, can't you do something about it? Ring them up and report it. The police. Yes. Yes. Tomorrow late. Yes. Ta. Love.

Robert replaces the receiver but does not turn round for a bit.

STELLA. What is it this time?

ROBERT. My car was stolen.

STELLA. How did she know where to find you?

ROBERT. I didn't ask her. – It was the Alfa, wouldn't have minded if it was the Fiat.

Stella walks out of the room. She goes outside and crosses the yard and climbs a wall. She walks towards the gable wall of an outhouse and stands by it, clawing at it.

Robert stands in the doorway, whistles. He sees no sign of her. He fetches a torch and shines it around. It takes him some time to locate Stella. He approaches her in the dark and shines the torch in her face. There is real panic in her expression.

ROBERT. I've made up my mind. – I'm going to leave her.

STELLA. There's no need to.

ROBERT. I know what it is to be happy, to actually like what you're doing and where you are and the woman you're with . . . To actually love it.

He dabs her face with his torch pretending to soak up her tears.

STELLA [*whisper*] Quench it, will you . . . I prefer to cry in the dark.

He quenches the torch and they stand there in the dark, enveloped by the enormous silence of the night.

Chapter Seventeen

When Robert enters the house with his suitcase, it is quiet and dim except for one light upstairs. He looks up, whistles, then calls.

ROBERT. Anybody home?

There is no reply but he does hear things being pitched around. He climbs the stairs, taking two steps at a time, and crosses the landing to his bedroom. Zee is pushing all his things into a tea-chest.

ZEE. It's time you got out, I mean we've had all we're ever going to have, the gravy as they call it.

She throws a clock, his shaving kit, clothes, shoes, everything, indiscriminately.

ROBERT. Where's my car?

ZEE. Get yourself a flat, or better still a mews. She can have window boxes.

ROBERT. What police station were you in touch with?

ZEE. Make sure the kitchen faces south, she'll be spending lots of time at her stove and her sink.

ROBERT. *Did they find it?*

ZEE. I'm afraid she'll get fat, I've watched her eat. In no time at all she'll be slopping around in bedroom slippers. I know how it will shape. And good luck to it. She'll want kids to make it fuller, to make it richer you understand, to hold it together. And of course you won't be able to give her any and you'll be going to doctors separately and together and you'll be having to drink to drown your sorrows, and then you'll notice little things about her, her breath, her armpits, her hair, the way her arches fall, and you'll have to get drunk before you go up the stairs to bed, that is if you have a stairs, if it's not all one level. You'll insist that she cut her hair, shave it, the way you did with me. But mine's growing, it's on the nape of my neck now.

ROBERT. It'll go with your broomstick. Maybe you just drove the car up the road a few miles, and dumped it there.

ZEE. Maybe I did.

ROBERT. If you did you'll be on crutches for quite a while.

ZEE. But you'll have to make sure first won't you, you wouldn't want to hurt me again and then find you'd done wrong. You'd be back in Wimpole Street at fifteen guineas a go. Why did I do it? Why am I destructive?

ROBERT. Where is it?

ZEE. How the hell would I know?

ROBERT. Is it smashed in?

He shakes her and lifts her off the ground.

ZEE. Getting it up eh . . . getting angrier, your good old presbyterian anger.

ROBERT. Tell me.

ZEE. Hit me and I will.

ROBERT. You scum. [*Slapping her fiercely*] I'll kill you.

There is an expression of victory on Zee's face.

ROBERT. No I won't . . . give you the satisfaction . . .

Robert throws her on the floor and rushes from the room. Zee rises, shakes herself to clear her head, runs to the hall and calls after him.

ZEE. Wait . . . wait . . .

Robert has already gone out the door. Zee runs back to her own bedroom and opens the window as high as it will go. She picks up the contents of the suitcase and dumps them out – things scatter in all directions.

ZEE. Bastard. Crook. Fraud. Woman-hater. Jew-hater.

Robert ignores both assaults and gets into her car and drives off recklessly, hooting to make sure she knows.

Zee is on the telephone dialling frantically.

When the telephone rings, Stella sits up, clicks on the light, and gropes for a minute before actually picking up the telephone.

ZEE. Is my husband in your lumpen proletarian arms?

STELLA. I beg your pardon.

ZEE. You needn't beg my pardon, baby, put me on to him.

STELLA. He's not here.

ZEE. I didn't think he would be. And before I get my fish stall and since you're on the blower there's a couple of things you ought to know, and you can start tearing your hair now, he's already chickening out, counting the cost, puking on my pillow, wondering how he'll get out of it and of course the more he wants to get out, the more he has to protest to you that he wants to get in. It's always like that with a cunt. Take my advice, skip it, you're not his type, you're not fun and games, you're a marvellous listener, but listening's dull in the sack, never made a marriage work, not his kind of marriage, you're a toddler as far as he's concerned, he likes a woman to be a mess, can't you see. That's why he's with me, he hates women. Oh, and another thing he hates is children. That's why we haven't got any. He'll be hell to your sons, give them complexes, he'll tell them they're too fat or too thin as the case may be, and you'll have to go to their bedroom at night to comfort them during their hols. and then you'll have to come down and pacify him. Between the devil and the deep sea.

Zee is suddenly shocked to find the phone has gone dead on her.

ZEE. Bitch. Vampire!

About dawn Robert emerges from a taxi. In the pathway he picks up whatever of his belongings he chances to find. There are others on the grass and on the rose bushes but he makes no attempt to rescue them. His mood is one of exhaustion. He enters his own house.

Zee is lying face down on her bed, naked. On the pillow next to her she has printed a large notice.

'THE PLACE TO PHONE IS WANDS-WORTH POLICE STATION'

ROBERT [*quietly*] Why couldn't you say so?

ZEE. You didn't give me a chance.

Robert is startled as she had the appearance of a sleeping person. She turns over and sits up, shielding her breasts with her hands. Her mood is calm, quiet, contrite.

ZEE. You tore into me, who has it, where is it, is it wrecked. I wasn't attacking. You were full of remorse about your dirty weekend, so you tore into me. You don't see yourself because you daren't. You don't see that you're going through hell and dragging me through hell and probably her. Poor cow.

ROBERT. Is it wrecked?

ZEE [*softly*] No no no. They said they have to hammer a few things out, a few dents.

Robert shakes his head wearily at her, at life, at the grim hour of the morning.

ROBERT. Well, I'll get a couple of hours sleep.

ZEE. Where's my mini?

ROBERT. It's at London Airport.

He takes a ticket and throws it on the bed.

ZEE. Can't we stop all this, all this wrangling, all this hell . . .

ROBERT. Yes. As from now. Call me at eight with some coffee.

Robert turns sharply and leaves the room with an air of finality. Zee's face is frightened, desperate, at last.

Chapter Eighteen

Stella and Robert are looking over a new unfurnished
flat. Stella goes from room to room saying Yoohoo
which echoes through the empty rooms.

STELLA. It can't be haunted because it's new,
nobody's lived here and nobody's died here.

ROBERT. We'll liven it up.

STELLA. You'll paint a wall, I don't mean house-
paint, I mean art.

ROBERT. From the Scottish school. Of course I will.

Robert taps the walls, examines the fittings, the
cupboards, the lintels etc.

ROBERT. We might have to put posts up to support
it.

Stella opens the french windows, walks on to a
small balcony.

STELLA. We can wave to the crowd.

ROBERT [*shyly*] It's not bad is it?

STELLA. Can it be pink and rosy?

ROBERT. It can be anything you want.

STELLA [*declamatory*] Do you snore? Do you grind
your teeth? Are there things about you I ought to
know? Are you a day or a night bug? Are you

irascible in the mornings?

Robert walks towards her, his arms outstretched. She meets him in the middle of the empty room and they start to dance.

ROBERT. Are you rich? Are you frigid? Are you an heiress, are you a whore?

They both start humming, their voices in first and seconds and they dance for a minute, oblivious of the fact that the house agent is in the doorway. The house agent waits, then coughs and they separate suddenly and shyly. Stella exits and Robert remains behind to discuss practicalities. Stella goes down the uncarpeted stairs and through the hallway.

When Robert gets to the car, Stella is sitting, crying quietly. They drive in silence for a bit.

ROBERT. I was going anyhow, for years. We discussed it. She went to her lawyer, I went to mine, she bought six houses, paid deposits on six houses, we had nothing to keep us, no bind, it wasn't as if we had kids or terrible financial worries. I think she'll get out of here altogether, go and live in the sun, she likes the sun.

STELLA. Somehow I don't ever see us as being perfectly happy.

ROBERT. I don't either, but we'll do our best.

Robert puts an arm around her and brings his cheek close to hers, and they drive like that, he thoughtful and she disconsolate.

Chapter Nineteen

Robert and Zee are playing table tennis again. Zee puts the bat down and walks towards the wall, disheartened. Robert stands and watches for a minute.

ROBERT. Are you all right?

Zee does not answer and Robert goes towards her, puts his hand on her back.

ZEE. Is it, was it, babies?

ROBERT. No, no no.

ZEE. But you'd like them. You get on with them.

ROBERT. I suppose so.

ZEE. That kid in your building, the Cypriot kid, does he still chat to you?

ROBERT. Yes, he has a bird now, a greenfinch, on his shoulder. Makes it do hoops and then for punishment he makes it go up and down stairs, hop, up and down seven flights of stairs.

ZEE. Can't we have a pet?

ROBERT. They die on us. One cat, one hamster and one canary, all in a row.

ZEE. That was our unlucky year.

ROBERT. Look, why don't I do something cheerful

for you? Take you up the street to that Italian place, it's new and it smells all right.

ZEE. I can't go out, I'm a mess.

ROBERT. You're not a mess.

Robert puts his arms around her. She rests her neck on his shoulder. He brings her over to a washbasin, turns on the tap and splashes her eyes.

ZEE. I'm your baby aren't I?

ROBERT. Yes you are.

ZEE [*timidly*] And I'll always be your baby, no matter whose lover you are or whose husband. – We should never have gone there, do you remember I had a hunch? I said Let's not go, and you said it would be unfair to Gladys. Well, damn Gladys.

Later at the restaurant, Robert is eating heartily, but Zee is not. There is a lighted candle on the table which she fiddles with.

ZEE. I was going to have my nose done, I thought that might help, but then I decided against it, it would need more than my nose. I sometimes think that though I have nice eyes, and I have, but they're not very friendly and I hate myself often and I wish I was old, not old gaga, but old, good, you know, like a woman in a chair with her family around her and her fruits and her flowers. I like night, it hides my ugliness, in my dreams I am not ugly, hardly ever. I often dream of people on bicycles, workmen and that, going by. I dreamt the other night that a workman offered me a bite of lunch. He had a bottle of water and believe it or not, a joint of roast beef, and we were in the middle of London somewhere, and he was carving me a bit of well-done roast beef. – What do you dream these days?

ROBERT. Oh the same things, mortar.

ZEE. You used to dream of a wolf. You said a wolf is dreaming me.

ROBERT. Oh yes, in the middle of nowhere.

ZEE. The wolf and you never met.

ROBERT. We always missed each other by a narrow shave, but we were going to meet, that was the whole point. That was the intention.

ZEE. We used to love the zoo. Sunday mornings. You did impersonations. You did a gorilla once and I got so scared I kept trying to make you stop and you went all gorillary, with arms and head.

Robert begins to do it again.

ZEE. No, it frightens me. Don't frighten me. Not now. Not tonight. – My husband is holding my hand under the cloth.

ROBERT. According to the news this evening, London is due for a small earth tremor.

ZEE. My husband is holding both my hands with both his hands . . .

ROBERT. Zee, Zee. Whereabouts are you now?

ZEE. Me?

ROBERT. You.

ZEE. I don't know. I sit in my car – our car – the one you gave me, and I think I'm getting separated from everyone I ever knew or loved. People don't like me you see, oh they like me but they hate me as well.

Women ask me to put on their eyelashes for them but they don't like me if you know what I mean. They don't trust me.

ROBERT. Nonsense.

ZEE. Do me the after-lunch people.

Robert does an impersonation of the boozy, after-lunch people in any street in London after lunch. The main thing is the eyes don't focus very well. If one eye looks up, the other eye does not correspond with it. Paunches are relaxed. He loosens the belt of his trousers for that. He signals hopelessly for a taxi. He impersonates a lahdidah voice.

ROBERT [*lahdidah voice*] Where am I? Where's Sloane Street, where's Harrods?

Now he is in a bookshop, he says, and lists some scintillating titles. He is appealing to the assistant.

ROBERT. I think you've got some books for me, you've put them aside, the name's Thompson, with a p, there's one supposed to be for a boy and one for a little girl. Could you write on the outside which is which.

Now Robert is talking to a group of protestors.

ROBERT. But what can I do, for humanity, for God, for the government. If only I could do something, 'Madam, so long as you don't eat white meat.' [*Normal voice*] I mean it's fantastic, you get the poisons working, the old enzymes, bumping into prams, wham, a pram in the middle of the road, more than one death, two, twins.

ZEE. No, we mustn't.

ROBERT. We mustn't laugh? We mustn't find the multitudes, idiot?

Robert and Zee kiss each other goodnight and are about to enter their separate bedrooms.

ZEE. Do you ever feel lonely with her too?

ROBERT. Yes.

Zee smiles but wearily and blows another kiss and closes her door.

In the throes of the night there is the noise of water running. Robert struggles with the decision whether to waken up or not. Suddenly he sits up in bed and clicks on the light. He gets out of bed and appears on the landing. The door leading to Zee's bedroom is open. He looks in and the tossed bed is empty. He crosses quickly to the bathroom door and tries to open it but it is locked. He tries the door again but in vain. He rushes downstairs and to the kitchen. From the cupboard he takes a tool box. He brings it with him and on the way up he hauls out a hammer. He breaks the lock and with his shoulder pushes the door in. The first thing he sights is Zee's wrists, gashed, in the bath of over-flowing blooded water.

Chapter Twenty

Robert is slouched on a chair in Stella's house. Stella is on another chair with a shawl round her. Robert has obviously been there for some short time.

ROBERT. Oh she'll live. She'll be all right. She'll be scarred.

STELLA. How do you mean, scarred?

Robert indicates slitting of a wrist, with his finger.

ROBERT. Kl . . . ee . . . hh.

STELLA. Oh my God, I thought she took pills.

ROBERT. She was so ashamed of herself when she came round.

STELLA. What did she say?

ROBERT. Nothing. She was distrait. Lost. Didn't know where she was. – She must love me quite a bit.

STELLA. Is that what you call it.

ROBERT. In a way . . . yes.

STELLA. Had you had a row, or something?

ROBERT. On the contrary. A bit of a laugh.

STELLA. Oh, a bit of a laugh.

ROBERT. For God's sake don't investigate, don't query it.

STELLA. I won't.

ROBERT. There's something I haven't told you.

We crashed once on a carriageway in Italy and I got her a doctor and he operated, on the road. They took everything out, her womb etcetera.

STELLA. Who was driving?

ROBERT. She was driving.

STELLA. Then it's not your fault.

ROBERT. Look, Missus, she nearly killed herself.

STELLA. What do you want me to do, cradle her? Go into mourning. Go to her, be with her. Hold her hand.

ROBERT. I don't want to hold her hand. The thought crossed my mind to let her die. I thought about it seriously for at least one minute, sixty seconds. I could have sat in the other room and let her bleed away, I could have. – If that makes you feel any the better.

Stella gathers the shawl around her for protection.

STELLA. There was a time when I didn't know either of you. You were just names, it was ages ago, I can't remember what I did then or who I was, or who I went out with.

ROBERT. I remember. I remember what I did then. I worked and I got drunk in the evenings, I went to a pub right next to my office.

STELLA. Where is she?

ROBERT. She's in St George's. The thing is she asked me to ask you, she wants to see you, [*He puts his hand up in a gesture of restraint*] no, no, not to complain, not to beseech, she just wants to see you, she likes you, you're the kind of woman she admires. She's never said it but she wishes she were you, you get things done, you have a serenity, keep your head above water.

STELLA. Serenity. I'm sick of serenity. I'm sick of the way I'm expected to be. I'd love to start this minute in another country, the Baltics, somewhere, and be a mess and be a child and be a bitch the way some women are. She wants me to be understanding and everyone thinks I'm O K. But I got short-changed too you know, I had a country and I left it, and I had a husband that I loved, yes I loved him and yes you are like him, the spitting image, we were happy, he and I, we could do crosswords and Scrabble and paper a room together, once I went into a shop and forgot he was in the car waiting and he waited three hours because I came out by another door and went home by taxi, I was pregnant at the time and a bit forgetful, he wasn't angry because we were as one. When they were infants he died and we knew he was going to die, he had a cancer but a mighty one, and he told me things that he would like to see done, qualities he would like to see instilled into his sons, journeys he would like us to make, we consulted maps together, the last thing he said was 'The front of the house and the woodwork need painting', and he didn't allow any tears, or any suicide or any ploys. I shut myself away but after a time I pieced myself together again and took up the threads and started the shop – we had to live – and started having dates and being in love again, or wanting to be in love, believe me it's nearly the same thing, and I've had the phone put down on me in the middle of the night too and I've slept with one of my pillows sideways so that I could imagine it was a man if I wakened up suddenly, until I came to my senses. Oh yes, I've let him down and I've let myself down. Once in a restaurant at Christmas time, in the late afternoon, there was fog on the window, in a restaurant near the Boltons, I asked a young man, a young man with blond hair, and dark eyelashes, I asked him to come to bed with me. I offered him money. I proposed by note and he just kept staring down into his cup of tea and I couldn't very well leave, because being Christmas time I was lumbered with all those packages. He was the one that had to leave without finishing his tea, or his bun.

ROBERT. People should never get to know each other too well.

STELLA. So I'm sorry to give the impression of being in charge. That's my mistake. I believe it's astrological, people born under my sign do. Nevertheless . . . I will always be all right. And so will you.

ROBERT. Yes?

STELLA. I shall hold on to my dream. And you shall too.

Robert rises.

ROBERT. But always alone, always.

She goes into the kitchen and starts to prepare some breakfast. She turns on all four jets of gas, also the oven, to warm the place. The shawl trails down her back and along the floor. He follows, sees her consternation, and then from behind, arranges the shawl more neatly around her shoulders.

Chapter Twenty-one

Zee is sitting up in bed, heavily bandaged, in a private ward of a hospital. Stella is sitting on the bed. Between them is a big basket of fruit which obviously Stella has brought. Zee is eating the grapes and spitting the pips into an envelope. Her aim is accurate.

ZEE. I'll plant them. You never know. They might take. You didn't know I liked gardening did you?

STELLA. He told me.

ZEE. Some people think plants have no nervous system. Personally I don't agree.

STELLA. He told me how you grew an avocado pear from a stone.

ZEE. He never told me anything about you except that sometimes he called me Stella. He slipped up.

STELLA. I got expelled because I fell in love with a nun. I embraced her when she was putting a mask on my face for the school play.

ZEE. I ate their altar breads or whatever they call them before they're blessed. What part did you play?

STELLA [*shyly*] I was a boy.

ZEE. You'll lend me him won't you?

STELLA. He's your husband.

ZEE. I mean for a week or two. It's going back to an empty house I can't bear.

STELLA. I know.

ZEE. Of course you do, you've been going back to an empty house for – how long?

STELLA. Long enough.

ZEE. Yes, it's your turn, it's in the stars. Your lucky period's coming up. Have you ever thought that you get your happiness at the expense of someone else, me of you, you of me, and so on and so forth.

STELLA. Did you plan it for a long time?

ZEE. No. It was a spur of the moment thing. We went out to dinner. I must have got sloshed. I have no intention of dying, I like it here, I like it more and more, I'm fine, I'm breathing better, breathing in and out, breathing out is very important, in case you don't know. It was a bit much of late, I mean even before you arrived on the scene it was a bit much. I didn't know whether to talk or be the silent type, we'd be looking at television and he'd put on his jacket and disappear and be gone for days, I don't know, he had some sort of bed in his office, I don't expect you've seen it, nobody's allowed to go there, especially not his nearest and dearest. And he has this very loyal assembly of ladies. He brings home the dirty linen. You'll be all right, you'll have a good time in the beginning, in the very beginning, the way people do. And I want you to, I'm sending vibrations that you shall, and you will 'cos my vibrations are very strong, they work. I can be your bridesmaid. I was my mother's bridesmaid for her third marriage, it wasn't intended but there was a train strike and the official bridesmaids' dresses didn't come, so I had to be a stand-in. We were miles away up country, in Kenya. I miss it, the baking sun, I like getting roasted, I do.

STELLA. Where is your mother?

ZEE. She lives in Johannesburg, for all the difference it makes . . . When I was eleven or twelve I had a bruise from a fall and I heard her say to her lover of the time, 'Ah, Zee's got her first lovebite'. I was in the swimming pool and they were lazying around.

Stella sees that there are tears in Zee's eyes. She pats her and feeds her the choicest grape.

ZEE. I've never told anyone that, not even him, no one knows but you.

Chapter Twenty-two

Robert is sleeping in a chair in his office, his shoes, socks and jacket on the floor. It is early morning and Rita enters with a cup of coffee and some pills. She puts the coffee down and to waken him breathes very gently on him. Her adoration is cloying. He wakens up, looks at her as she hands him the pills, he groans.

RITA. Vitamins.

She takes a face flannel and pats it over his face and forehead. He lies back with the flannel over his face and sips the coffee.

ROBERT. What's nervous breakdown? Is it when you can't make up your mind?

RITA. It's when you act out of context with your environment and you . . .

Robert puts his hand up to restrain her.

ROBERT. Don't tell me . . . Don't give me any definitions. Do men get it?

RITA. One of my beaux did. He started ordering things mail order, had this fetish about having things clean, underwear, mine, his.

ROBERT [*interrupting*] I don't seem to be able to come through for either of them. They met, they had grapes, muscat grapes as I understand it.

RITA. You're doing fine, just fine.

Robert removes the flannel from his face for a glance.

ROBERT. Could you be a little less, optimistic. You remind me of everyone's mother during the war, breezy. That's what I need, a war, in the trenches, locks of hair, souvenirs.

He places the flannel over his face and basks for a moment in the comfort of it.

Rita begins to weep first silently, then sniffles.

ROBERT. Now don't tell me you're crying.

He waits for a moment before removing the face flannel.

ROBERT. Sit, sit down. Did some cad stand you up last night?

RITA. No, I go with John steady now.

ROBERT. There's nothing worse is there?

He puts his hand out and taps her on the shoulder, does a funny accent.

ROBERT. It's a funfair, that's what it is, love. You put your money and you take your chances.

RITA. I mean I have everything, a nice flat and central heating and John comes every evening.

ROBERT. And do you come every evening?

Rita goes on crying.

ROBERT. You can tell me. Go on, spout. You can tell me anything, any time, provided I listen.

RITA. You remember the night you came to my house to pick up the specification?

ROBERT. Yes.

RITA. Do you?

ROBERT. Yes. A cul-de-sac. Couldn't turn my car around. You made me an omelette, a herb omelette.

RITA. I had no whisky. You had to drink beer. You put salt in your beer. You were the first person I ever saw put salt in his beer. You put salt on your hand for me to lick, the saltlick you said. To give one a thirst. You said sometimes you could taste things out of the blue, parsnips, and mushrooms and all sorts of tastes. Likewise smell.

ROBERT. You've got an incredible memory.

RITA. About some things.

ROBERT. Someone asked me the other day, my tailor as a matter of fact, if your wife and your mistress were drowning who would you save. I said my wife because my mistress would understand.

RITA. You're wrong. Neither of them would.

ROBERT. Why can't it *all* be kept trivial?

They look at each other for the first time.

ROBERT. I'll come back some time, some time.

Robert is visiting Zee in the hospital ward.

ROBERT. You're looking better. Your colour's good.

ZEE. They give me iron. It's like being young again.

ROBERT. Could they give me a few drams?

ZEE. Can I ask you something?

ROBERT [*hedging*] Well, you're going to, so you might as well.

ZEE. Can we have a party? Announce it to everyone. 'We're breaking up.' That'll shake 'em.

ROBERT. They know.

ZEE. Yes, but this way 'twill have balls. I won't feel ditched.

ROBERT. You're not ditched. You'll never be ditched. You'll always have more friends than me, and more admirers.

ZEE. I'll pay for it. I'll sell my emerald.

ROBERT. No you won't.

ZEE. Then we can.

ROBERT. But what's the point.

ZEE. I'd like it. That's the point. That's the only point. They all think I'm getting my come-uppance, your brothers and Gladys and your accountant and all our dear friends.

ROBERT. What would they know about us. Only we know that.

ZEE. I'll have her later for lunches and brunches and things but the party is . . . ours.

Zee puts her hand out and he places his over it and she puts her other hand over his and they play the game of hands with mounting speed.

Chapter Twenty-three

Stella and Robert are in the half-furnished flat. Stella is unpacking crystal glasses and taking them out one by one and holding them up to make sure they are not blemished. Robert is putting a modern kitchen table together.

ROBERT. Are they Venetian or something?

STELLA. Something. Will we have a house-warming?

ROBERT. If you want.

STELLA [*rueful*] But we don't have any mutual friends.

ROBERT. Yes we have, your kids.

STELLA. You know what Shaun said, he said 'Please indicate to Robert that great favour is curried with material offerings from a step-father'.

ROBERT. Cheek. I'll send him a curt ten shilling note.

STELLA. And I've made a number of resolutions. I'll be less extravagant. I won't talk in the mornings. I'm an early riser. But on Sunday mornings I lie in, and read the papers and eat toast. I won't have a head-cold ever.

Robert comes close behind her and puts his arm around her. She has a glass in her hand. He raises it up as if there was a drink in it.

ROBERT. We're a party in ourselves.

STELLA. I wish we were sleeping here tonight.

ROBERT. It's not set up.

STELLA. We could sleep on the floor . . .

ROBERT. I get a crick in my neck . . .

STELLA. Or I can make the bed up, I can . . . easily.

ROBERT. Look, she invited a couple of people, old friends and relations, it's my last sort of bowing-out night.

Stella turns away and drinks bitterly from the empty glass that is in her hand.

STELLA. Well, I'm staying . . .

ROBERT. Why?

STELLA. To christen the place.

ROBERT. On your own?

STELLA. On my own.

Robert makes a gesture to leave. She does not shake hands with him. He kisses her hair.

ROBERT. It's not something I'm looking forward to.

He strokes her gently, then on tiptoe, leaves.

Zee's farewell party is in full swing. There is a hired orchestra. There is one long table laid with food. On another table Zee is dancing wildly. She is wearing a long silk dress with slits at either side. The dress has sleeves with elasticated ends and sometimes she

submerges her hands in them and does funny movements with her arms. Several of the guests are watching, enraptured. Robert enters and Zee jumps off the
table and through the crowd to greet him.

ZEE. Here's my feller.

In the flat Stella is trying to put a brass bed together.
She is trying to link the two ends with a long metal
bar. Naturally the span of her arms is not enough to
keep both ends upright at the same moment, and just
as she manages to screw the bar into one end the
other falls. She is not seen to be sad, just frustrated.

At Zee's party some are dancing and some are eating.
A pretty girl is reading a man's hand. She has the
hand positioned in her crotch but appears to be
reading intently. Gladys is observing the various
tattoos on a young man's chest and arms. Robert is
sitting on the arm of a chair and beside him are Zee,
and Ted, a good-looking man of about thirty. Zee has
the whisky bottle under her arm. She is about to drink
from it.

ZEE. Down the hatch.

Robert takes the bottle from her but before he has
time to drink she brings her mouth to his and gives
him what she has just imbibed. He is surprised. A new
game.

ZEE. That's what the birds do.

ROBERT [*with a smile*] Yeh . . .

ZEE. To their young.

TED [*holding an empty glass*] What kind of party is this?

Robert fills the glass quickly. He puts an inordinate amount in. The whisky goes glug, glug, glug.

ROBERT. A drinking party, given by my wife.

Zee takes the full glass from Ted, puts it on a table.

ZEE [*to Ted*] My hips are going wild, do you mind?

Zee and Ted start to dance. Robert looks up, a bit baffled, a bit jealous. The girl who has been reading hands crosses over and takes his hand to read it. He declines.

ROBERT. I don't want to know. I don't want to know. I don't want to know. [*Differing his tone of voice for each time he says it*].

The brass bed is upright. Stella is in the process of putting the spring frame on it. She hauls it across the floor, rests for a minute. She has that concentrated expression of someone who is talking to herself, deliberating on what she must do.

Robert has taken up the full glass of whisky which Zee left on a table and is drinking it purposefully. He does it as if drinking with one of the boys, that is, he makes a big show of it. He has his right elbow jutted out and his shoulder raised accordingly and he is knocking it back. Gladys is standing in front of him.

GLADYS. They're fun people.

ROBERT. Sure, sure.

GLADYS. Never been so flattered in all my life. Just now he said, 'Who's the bird?' . . . me!

ROBERT. Of course you're a bird, you're all birds . . . alas.

Robert puts down the glass, takes her in his arms and dances with her, but already showing signs of stumbling. Close up of Gladys's face as she makes a signal to Zee who is also dancing. Zee and Ted join with Gladys and Robert and they all link arms and dance some improvised thing. Robert is laughing a lot and is out of step.

Stella has made up the bed and is putting a lace cover over it. Then she draws back the cover and lies on the bed to try its comfort and reliability. She lies on one side, then moves to the other, trying to decide which suits her best. She rises and goes to the mirror and starts to undress. She touches her lonely body, her throat, one breast, then the other. She looks at her watch, then picks up a small travel clock and brings it to her ear to see if it is working. She winds it and sets the alarm button.

Robert is helped on to a chair by Zee and Ted. He is fast asleep. Zee starts to take off his boots. She does it very slowly, so as not to disturb him.

TED. First sign of cracking up.

ZEE. Ssshh ...

Ted tries to help with the other boot but Zee doesn't allow him. She gestures with index finger, in a walking pattern, that he go. Ted waits for a minute. Zee has taken off both boots and put them side by side. They look foolish, as does Robert, slumped there.

ZEE [*whisper*] Isn't he lovely ...

Zee follows Ted to the door and waves to him and others who are in the hallway. They leave without closing the hall door. Zee doesn't bother to. She returns to Robert's side, closing the study door first. She loosens Robert's tie, then his shirt buttons. Then comes the big operation. She lifts him from the chair on to the floor, on to a soft sheepskin rug. She removes his jacket. She shakes it for sounds of keys and money. She looks to see how asleep he is. She takes out one bunch of keys which are ones we will have already seen as being those of his office, house, cars, etc. Then she takes out another, a new bunch, two very new keys on a string with a label attached, the keys to Stella's flat. She puts them safely in her handbag. Then she clicks out the light, undresses hurriedly, is seen to be wearing nothing, not even a pair of pants, under her long dress. She lies next to Robert and opens the buttons of his trousers, then the zip. The noise of the zip is the only sound in the darkness. She hauls the trousers down as far as his knees and then mounts him.

Stella is in her bed sleeping. Her bedroom door is opened and she sits up, saying 'Robert'.

STELLA. Robert, is that you, Robert?

Stella clicks on the light with one hand and with the other starts to take out some clips with which she has pinned her hair. It is a strange man. We shall call him Bert.

STELLA. What are you doing in my bedroom?

BERT. Just helping myself.

He approaches her with some rope and ties her hands behind her back. He is quite pleased with her appearance, leers at her.

BERT. Just routine.

Bert then goes to her dressing table, picks up ear-rings, the jewellery box, various oddments.

STELLA. I always thought you worked in pairs.

BERT. Not me, I'm a loner.

He opens various drawers, the wardrobe, takes out her dresses, takes out her mink jacket which he strokes. Stella watches at first in silence. From time to time he diverts his attention from the clothes to her. Will he molest her? She tries to be off-hand.

STELLA. When did you start?

BERT. Can't remember. – As a kid I suppose, I raided orchards.

STELLA. I bet there were broken bottles on the wall, broken green bottles.

BERT [smiling] Yeh. I'd forgotten that.

Bert starts examining her jewellery, looking at it carefully through a magnifying glass.

STELLA. That ring, I'd mind most about it. It has what they call sentimental value.

BERT. That's what they all say.

STELLA. Were you inside?

BERT. Yeh, they always put me in psychiatric. – Do you live alone?

STELLA. I have done.

BERT. Sorry, I didn't mean to be personal.

STELLA. Go ahead, be personal. I'm expecting someone tomorrow, or half-expecting, and he wants to come, and I want him to come, but there's more than that to it and I'm telling you all this because I'm in a state and you've been in psychiatric and I don't often get in a state, believe me, these are exceptional times, strange times these are.

Bert walks towards her. There is a moment's tension as to what he is going to do.

BERT. You oughtn't to live alone you know. – It's morbid.

Bert touches the patchwork quilt on her bed, feels it, admires it, gives her one sinister slow look then returns and puts all the things he has stolen on to it. Stella lies rigid as he ties it into a bundle and knots it carefully. He bounces it a bit to mime farewell.

BERT. You'll be all right, he'll come.

STELLA. Did you take the ring?

BERT. Yeh, it's the best, the most valuable thing.

Bert goes.

STELLA. I don't think I will be all right. I don't think I will be all right.

She sits there lolling her head back and forth, repeating the phrase.

Robert wakens, looks around, sees that Zee is lying beside him with a shawl over her, her arms, hair etc. entwined in his. He raises his head a fraction to see that he has been partly undressed. He can guess the rest. He rises. His hangover is bad, so is his remorse. He rises, drags his clothes on and goes from the room, making a lot of noise.

He goes to the kitchen and throws out the remainder of the champagne. But that is not enough. He opens full bottles of beer, a bottle of gin, and does the same. He is surprisingly vengeant. His intent is that not a drop of drink be left in the house. He throws the bottles into the adjoining sink.

Then he goes upstairs to pack. His actions are quick and careless. He throws shirts in, on their hangers Zee enters with the shawl wrapped around her. She too is cold, hungover and in need of comforting. Her mood changes as soon as she appraises the situation.

ZEE. Where are you going?

ROBERT. Off. O . . . F . . . F.

ZEE. But you're not. Last night you changed your plans.

ROBERT. I can imagine.

ZEE. You begged me, you asked me . . .

Robert continues packing.

ZEE. If only you knew the things you said. – You

said, save me Zee. – You said, help me Zee. –
You made me promise.

ROBERT. In my cups.

ZEE [*innocent voice*] You crossed your heart.

ROBERT. Well, I'm uncrossing it.

Zee goes and crosses her fingers over his heart
several times, determined now.

ZEE. Don't go, please don't go today, wait, wait
till I get someone, a lodger, or an au pair, anyone.

Robert turns away and tries to continue with his
packing. As quickly as he puts the things in the case
she takes them out again and they tug at either end
of his 'Stella' shirts.

ZEE. Don't leave me alone in the house. I'm frightened. I'm afraid of the dark.

ROBERT. Keep the lights on.

ZEE. You're not going, you can't go.

ROBERT. You know I'm going. It's a *fait
accompli* . . .

The shirt gets torn as he grabs it from her. He looks
at it, then stoops down and uses it to shine his shoes.
He is trying to be both calm and cursory.

ROBERT. And there is nothing you can do about
it – You've had the last drop of me, or whatever you
had, in the night.

Zee starts hitting his back, hitting wildly.

ZEE. Fool. Why do you think she isn't shacked up
long ago with someone, she's presentable enough
when clad, and she's got cash, why do you think she's
alone.

ROBERT. She's discriminating, that's why.

ZEE. Discriminating shit. She's all loused up and it takes a gink like you not to see through her.

ROBERT [*straightening up*] But you do.

ZEE. Yes I do.

ROBERT. What are you talking about?

ZEE. Peruse it ... I've eaten and drunk with her, I've had fittings ...

ROBERT. It won't work baby.

ZEE. It has worked ... Baby.

ROBERT. Jesus ...

ZEE. Call her up, get her around.

ROBERT. You'd fuck anything.

ZEE. Sure I would ... she'll be dried up soon enough and then it'll be back to prossies time and the penicillin bit like before you met me and it'll be ever so excruciating, you've been luckier than you realize, getting your juices here and spewing it out there. By God, you'll need me, you'll need me like you've never done.

ROBERT. Never ...

ZEE. And by God I'll be there.

Robert stands and observes her very quietly.

ROBERT. Finished?

ZEE. For the time being ... yeh.

Robert takes a slipper and starts to beat her, quietly and viciously.

ZEE. Not my face, not my face, not my face ...

It is indeed her face he beats, mercilessly.

Chapter Twenty-four

Stella is sitting beside the telephone, head down. There is a ring at the doorbell. She opens the door and Robert enters.

ROBERT. You weren't at the shop.

It takes him a second to realize that she is angry.

ROBERT. What's the long face for?

STELLA. She couldn't wait to ring me. 'Have I wakened you Stella, this is Gladys, you missed a marvellous evening, one of the great evenings.'

ROBERT. Well you didn't.

STELLA. She said you danced the Charleston with each other.

ROBERT. I don't know what I danced. I was pissed.

STELLA. Maybe you'd like to rethink the whole situation.

ROBERT. Yeh, that's why I'm here.

STELLA. You lied to me, no one lies to me, not even my own children.

ROBERT. It wasn't a lie, it had nothing to do with you, the course of the evening. – Space . . . that's what we promised each other. Remember? All those grand phrases.

STELLA. Who wanted me to move, who got me to leave my own house where I have lived the best of myself?

ROBERT. It wasn't big enough.

STELLA. For me.

ROBERT. For a *family*.

STELLA. I'll believe it when you bring your belongings.

ROBERT. Nothing's different . . . I'm coming.

STELLA. When?

ROBERT. Soon.

STELLA. On a stretcher.

ROBERT. Don't be fatalistic.

STELLA. Stringing her along, giving her hope.

ROBERT. I'm giving her nothing, except money.

STELLA. Oh yes you are. You're keeping it going by hook or by crook. It's a spell you can't be parted from.

ROBERT. It's bile.

STELLA. Get rid of it!

ROBERT. What do you suggest? Carter's Little Liver Pills, suicide. Come on nurse, nanny, Nightingale.

STELLA. Last night you had a party, the night before you had to tuck her in, tonight she will have to be read to, I hope it's a fairy tale and that you cuddle up.

ROBERT. We have separate rooms, you know that. You've asked often enough in your empirical way.

STELLA. I don't care what you have, separate

rooms, beds, gas ovens, I don't want her name bandied round here and her wants, and her wrists, and her berserks. Maybe she'd like me to sit at the end of the bed tonight, to honour the proceedings.

ROBERT. Yeh. . . maybe. You had a few encounters.

STELLA [*she holds the door open*] Don't let me detain you.

ROBERT. I can stay for a bit.

STELLA. I don't want to see you like this and I don't want to be seen like this. You're everything I ever despised and I'm everything I vowed not to be. That's where our love has got us to.

He walks towards the door and stands on the threshold.

ROBERT. I didn't set out to fall in love with you, I set out to have an affair, a little on the side, the sort of thing a man wants, but I fell in love with you, it happened precisely, if you want to know, that evening with your kids. I sat at the table and wham! I fell in love with a household. I felt like I'd come home, I'd arrived. That's the way it happened and that still stands. All these other things, my life, her life, it's all junk, and I don't want it but I've got it.

Robert starts to walk away.

STELLA [*overcalmly*] I wish now that you'd let her die.

ROBERT. *You* wish it.

Stella closes the door and locks it. She starts to pack her dresses into an open trunk.

Robert is trying on various engagement rings. He selects one and tries it on the shop assistant, who is a young girl.

YOUNG GIRL. What size sir?

ROBERT. Ah . . . mmm, your size. – I can always change it.

YOUNG GIRL. Usually the couple . . .

ROBERT. I don't believe it!

He looks at the various price tags.

ROBERT. Pricey, aren't they?

YOUNG GIRL. Well, they're diamonds . . .

He takes the one he had her fit on. He is in a hurry to get out of there.

Stella is still wandering around in her nightgown, gathering bits and pieces. The doorbell rings, a tiny, friendly tinkle and just as it rings, the key is turned in the latch and Zee enters. Her face is very bruised. She is carrying a little basket.

ZEE. It's only me . . . Forgive my scars.

Zee crosses the room, eagerly, taking stock of it.

ZEE [*indicating the curtains*] Ah, all web, all dreamy.

STELLA. You – trespasser.

ZEE. I brought you a little present, a little creature to keep you company.

Zee lifts the cloth off the basket and presents it to Stella. The cat's head and snout peer forward. Stella backs away.

STELLA. Christ.

ZEE. She's a she.

STELLA. Get her out of here.

ZEE. I had her nails pared. So she won't scratch.

STELLA. Get out.

As Stella retreats Zee pursues her.

ZEE. Stella! It's the easiest thing in the world, a little kitten, a fear of [*with her index finger touches Stella*] Go on touch it, chance it.

STELLA. I don't want to.

At once Zee puts the lid on the basket and puts the basket out of the way, near the door. She murmurs something affectionate to it. She rises, goes towards Stella.

ZEE. All right, you don't want to. Fine.

Stella eludes her by walking towards the door which is already half open, and opens it wide.

STELLA. Have you finished?

Zee pays no notice of that but picks up some object that she admires.

ZEE. I used to be afraid of everything, including kittens, and my father gave me a fantastic piece of advice, he said if ever you're frightened of anything, grab hold of it. I used to be afraid of my nipples. [*she touches her own breasts rather casually*] You've got to like yourself, that's the crux of it, I don't think you like yourself.

STELLA. I don't like you.

ZEE [*wagging a finger at her*] You do.

STELLA. I never have.

ZEE. If it weren't for him we'd be chums.

STELLA. I doubt it.

ZEE. I'd have you casing London with tigers on your shoulders.

Instinctively Stella starts to walk very straight as if she had a book on her head.

STELLA. I'm fine.

ZEE. You're not fine. And you're not going to be fine . . . that's what it's all about, you want to live with him in your little box, Old Mother Hubbard. You ought to know better.

STELLA. You didn't give him very much rope.

ZEE. I do now. *And* I'm giving you rope. I've hit rock bottom, don't forget, last week.

STELLA. Oh, the epitaph as you would say.

ZEE [*coming nearer to her*] Why are you shaking?

STELLA. I detest scenes.

Stella goes to the door and kicks the basket out. Noise off of cat's miaow.

ZEE. Suppose I refuse to go.

STELLA. Then I'll go.

ZEE. I'll follow you.

Again instinctively Stella starts to walk back into the room and into the fracas.

STELLA. Why? Why? He's finished with you.

ZEE. You don't want to miss out on anything. You don't want to be deceived.

STELLA [*much too jealously*] How then?

Zee goes towards her and does an imaginary punch in her direction, but is smiling.

ZEE. No-one's deceiving you, baby. They couldn't,

you make beautiful dresses, and people love you.

Zee now makes a sweep round the room, opening everything that is openable, cupboards, windows, wardrobe door, everything.

ZEE. Open up! . . . Whoooom . . . Whooooom, take a chance. Let it happen.

As quickly as Zee opens these things, Stella runs to close them and there is the alternate image and sound of things being opened and closed, violently.

ZEE. That's what I want for you.

STELLA. Want, shit.

Zee comes behind Stella, who has just closed the wardrobe door with a thud, touches her lightly on the waist and starts humming.

ZEE. Let's dance.

Zee steers Stella into a dance as she sings.

ZEE [*singing*] Beautiful dreamer, awake unto me, Starlight and dewdrops are waiting for thee . . . When in doubt . . . dance. That's my motto.

She looks at Stella expecting a reply but gets none. She puts her forefinger on the indent of Stella's upper lip.

ZEE. Do you know why you have that?

Stella answers just by nodding her head.

ZEE. Just before you're born an angel puts its finger there to tell you to keep still. You do, you're the silent type.

Zee makes a kissing sound.

ZEE. Give us a kiss.

Stella is stonefaced.

ZEE [*like a child*] It's only a gas.

While still dancing Zee gets up on her toes and gives Stella a peck.

ZEE. But a nice gas.

They continue to dance and we see their two faces, Zee's very gay and Stella bewildered but glad to be dancing because at least it involves movement and she allows herself to spin. Zee's voice becomes softer as the dancing continues.

ZEE. You know the marvellous thing about women? [*pause*] [*whisper*] They've got an extra chromosome. [*pause*] You don't dislike me really. [*pause*] You don't dislike anyone. [*pause*] You couldn't, with your heart.

Zee looks up and sees Stella's tears.

ZEE. Don't cry. [*pause*] Or do cry. [*pause*] Do anything you want. [*pause*] You never thought we'd touch, did you? [*pause*] Well neither did I. [*pause*] And it's lovely. And the lights are all smoky, and the orchestra, the orchestra's lovely, dreamy. [*pause*] Make a wish.

To her surprise Stella speaks, and her voice is very clear, somewhat hypnotic, as if she too believed in the illusion that has just been presented to her.

STELLA. I would just dance and make love all my life.

ZEE. You shall. You will.

They dance a little more robustly now with Stella leading. Stella continues the song.

STELLA [*singing*] Gone are the cares, Of life's busy throng, Da da da da da, da da da da.

ZEE. They're much the same, dancing and making love.

Stella commences another kind of dance, a quickstep, and sings.

STELLA [*singing*] Give me land lots of land, Neath the starry skies above, Don't fence me in . . .

ZEE. Hold me. Hold me.

STELLA. Silly girl.

ZEE. Yes I'm silly. I want you to hold me. I want to be held in your arms.

Stella holds her as if she were a child.

ZEE. More, more, more.

Zee crouches a little and while being held she kisses Stella's body.

Stella runs her hand through Zee's hair, gently, languid almost. They are standing in such a way that Zee is facing the door.

ZEE [*as she clings to Stella*] You don't know your powers you don't.

STELLA. There there there.

ZEE. You're going to possess us both.

STELLA. Both?

ZEE [*in a whisper*] He's here.

Stella turns and looks. Zee still clings to her. Robert enters, picks up the basket and crosses the room. Stella puts her hand out and as he sees her face he sees she is full of emotion.

ROBERT. You lovely, lovely woman.

ZEE. She is.

ROBERT [*whispers*] I'm back.

Together they embrace and start to kiss slowly and lovingly, Robert and Zee begin to undress Stella.

ZEE [*whisper*] He's back . . . We're back . . . We're all together . . . Back . . . As it was in the beginning . . . is now . . . and ever shall be . . . World without end . . . Amen.

Over the action of her whisper they have slipped out of their shoes, and with her foot Zee has lifted the lid of the basket and put Stella's foot on top of the kitten and her own foot to secure it there. The last we see are their three bodies – arms, heads, torsos, all meeting for a consummation.

Edna O'Brien

'Miss O'Brien is an expert on girls and their feelings.
... No writer in English is so good at putting the reader
inside the skin of a woman' – *Evening Standard*

The Country Girls

This famous first novel introduces two delightful
heroines, Kate and Baba, and a host of other Irish
characters in unpredictable situations.

Girl with Green Eyes

The comic and poignant sequel to *The Country Girls* in
which Caithleen Brady finds romance in Dublin –
classy romance with the second Mr Gentleman.

Girls in their Married Bliss

Readers of the previous two novels will not be
surprised at the tragicomedy of the married lives of
Kate and Baba.

Casualties of Peace

Willa had loved and been hurt by love so she tried to
build her world with the faithful Tom and Patsy to
shut out the threat of feeling. But the tension mounts
until eventually it is bound to snap . . .

August is a Wicked Month

Ellen was alone in London, separated from her husband.
Bored and frustrated, she decided to go south in search
of sun and sex – but it was not quite as easy as that.

The Love Object

Each of Edna O'Brien's heroines, in these short stories,
swings, in her different way, between susceptibility and
scepticism, euphoria and agonizing disappointment.

Not for the sale in the U.S.A.